The

Sharman ⟨Macdonald was born in⟩
Glasgow ⟨and grew up in⟩
Edinburgh. ⟨After⟩
leaving ⟨Edinburgh University⟩ she
moved to London to work as an
actress. Her first play, *When I was a
Girl, I Used to Scream and Shout . . .*,
was performed at the Bush Theatre,
London, in November 1984, then at
the Lyceum Theatre, Edinburgh, as
part of the 1985 Edinburgh Festival,
and subsequently at the Whitehall
Theatre, London, in 1986. Sharman
Macdonald was awarded the 1984
Standard Award for the most
promising playwright and the Thames
Television Bursary to be writer in
residence at the Bush Theatre. She is
married to actor Will Knightley and
has two children.

Also by Sharman Macdonald

When I was a Girl, I Used to Scream and Shout . . .
(Faber & Faber)

Sharman Macdonald
The Beast

Flamingo
Published by Fontana Paperbacks

First published in Great Britain by
William Collins Sons & Co. Ltd 1986
This Flamingo edition first published
in 1987 by Fontana Paperbacks
8 Grafton Street, London W1X 3LA

Flamingo is an imprint of
Fontana Paperbacks, part of
the Collins Publishing Group

Copyright © Sharman Macdonald 1986

Made and printed in Great Britain by
William Collins Sons & Co. Ltd, Glasgow

Conditions of Sale
This book is sold subject to
the condition that it shall not, by
way of trade or otherwise, be lent,
re-sold, hired out or otherwise
circulated without the publisher's
prior consent in any form of binding
or cover other than that in which it
is published and without a similar
condition including this condition
being imposed on the
subsequent purchaser

Roger withdrew from Jade. Not her real name of course, adopted after the sixties in honour of the Jade Emperor, whoever he was. Jade admired power. Passively. She was very small. Roger jack-knifed his body and swung his legs over the edge of the bed. A fat man who dreamed that he maintained a reputation for fitness. With surprising speed, for all his bulk, the fat man moved, light on his feet; that sort of thing. He was studying astral projection, the ultimate in weight loss without diet. Jade untied the knot of her hair from round his neck. It grew down past her waist and tipped the groove of her backside. Roger had nightmares about that hair, suffocating in the great mud mass of it. Nevertheless on Sunday mornings he tied it round his neck to make love. Jade insisted that Roger love her hair, told everyone that he would not have her cut it off. Bully that he was. Men.

He padded off the bed into the bathroom, picked up the natural sponge, supermarket purchase on a bleached Mediterranean rock, two hundred pesetas and worth it; they'd bought several and some for their friends. Picked up the Evian water atomizer and the cream. Jade hated to be dry, hated to be sticky, refused to pollute the hormonious workings of her body with hormonious additives, abhorred the insertion of foreign copper matter into her soft privacy, eschewed the bubblegum alternative and wanted no child. They established a rhythm and he withdrew. Jade hated the smell of sperm. He'd forgotten to wipe himself. He used a shammy leather rubbed with Silvikrin's soft alternative to soap and dabbed himself dry with the small towel, his towel, dabbed, not rubbed. Dip dab dab. Dip dab dab. He couldn't get down to sniff any lingering odour of Sunday morning emissions. He didn't bend like that. There were soft rubber bands of white flesh at his waist. His stomach was the hanging bag of a used-up pregnancy. He didn't bend. He faced his Sunday morning creased ugliness, saluted to chase away the demons and took the Evian water to the bedroom.

Jade drawled a soft complaint at the slowness of his progress from bedroom to bathroom and back again. She had practised the soft complaint since joining the Peace Movement. Until then, hers had been the strident voice of the girl turned irretrievably woman and resenting it. Jade was beautiful. Jade was beautiful. It was part of the Sunday morning ritual that Roger should clean his sperm from the purity of her belly, retrieve any gasping its last in the thickness of her pubic hair, so unpleasant if it caked dry there. Roger wiped her with the sponge. Dip dip dab. Dip dip dab. They waited for her to dry in the good air.

'Thank God it's summer,' she said.

The breeze sifted through the net curtain, net not lace. Jade liked plastic, sponge and nylon.

'Thank God it's summer.'

Man-made materials used in the face of a generation returning to raw wood, Jade construed as style. They drank from red plastic and had fresh salads from red plastic bowls on a black plastic table. The flowers, fresh cut and stark without leaves, lived and died in white plastic vases. Roger sprayed Jade's stomach with Evian water. She giggled deliciously. The delicious giggle had always been a part of their Sunday morning ritual. The Evian water was an innovation. After the giggle, she held up her face, eyes closed, and he sprayed that too. They waited for her to dry. Her position on the bed was the relaxed pose of a woman sated by love. She'd taken it from an Ingres nude. Jade had never had an orgasm, did not miss them. She was sure you never missed what you ... Roger with supple, gentle fingers rubbed the 'without cruelty to animals' cream for the body and the hands into Jade's stomach; she turned over, he rubbed it into her buttocks, down the crease, up her back. Roger took care of Jade's beauty.

'Only one of us is beautiful here,' he'd say, and in

company he'd run his hand down the length of her hair, kiss the inside of her wrist. He cherished Jade's beauty. They lay side by side for ten minutes upon the bunk five foot by six in the room six foot by seven. One always had to be so tidy in a small flat. In the storage space underneath the sponge mattress lay everything they had in the world which could not be displayed. The first summer air blew upon Jade's buttocks and fanned Roger's cheeks.

In the kitchen, while Roger blew dry what was left of his hair, Jade boiled potatoes and mixed mayonnaise and chives for a potato salad. She never made her own mayonnaise, Hellman's was so absolutely marvellous, though she did add a touch of lemon, a splash of paprika and a trickle of tabasco. Her salads were famous. The prawns she'd defrosted the night before. Kraft's seafood dressing, a red plastic bowl and a squitter of grapefruit juice. She opened the window from the kitchen onto their balcony garden. It was three feet wide and six feet long. Enough room for two chairs and some potted plants. They'd hauled the potting compost up the two flights of stairs and onto the balcony together. It was backbreaking work. They'd christened the balcony 'garden' and entertained their friends with tales of planting endeavours. They'd drawn out scaled plans of plants on graph paper, painted them in pastel water-colour, put them in black plastic frames and hung them as a display upon the wall. Roger put his arms around Jade and they sighed together on the balcony of their love. The railings had cost five hundred pounds. One had to be safe.

Roger's face was smooth and creamed. Roger's hair was pallid silk. Their picnic friends had a child. Roger was nervous of children but sensible enough not to wear his white boiler suit. He iiked himself in white. The gleaming reflection from the stark cotton pulled the lines from his face and gave him a baby bland Churchillian dignity. He went to the delicatessen to buy beef and kabanos for their vegetarian picnic friends. Beef very finely sliced and red in the middle. Jade and Roger chose to have a Baby Belling in their kitchen seven foot six by three. The Baby Belling sat on top of the fridge, half size, so Roger always bought his white wine ready chilled and his beef ready cooked.

Roger loved Hampstead. He loved Sunday Hampstead. A take-away Provençal restaurant had opened with discreetly blinded windows so that your guests would assume that dinner came from your own kitchen and not François down the road. Roger liked knowing that business would not suffer from value added tax. Roger planned a French candle-lit meal from the Provençal take-away and looked at a white voile blouse which would expose Jade's nipples. The boutique was open but he would not buy clothes on a Sunday. Positively. He put down a deposit. Reserved it. Would pick it up on Monday evening. Tomorrow would still be summer.

The lady of the delicatessen was washing her hands as Roger pushed open the door. She washed her hands between beef and cheese, between salami and salmon mousse. She was meticulous and sullen. If there was a queue it moved slowly. Roger always treated her with perfect politeness. He smiled and ducked and bobbed and weaved, his baby face glistened and shone and blushed purple pink. He oozed bashful charm. His reward was a slight lessening of the Italian-browed frown and a lifting of the moustachioed top lip. She was a lady untouched by beauty even in her youth and Roger loved her for her salads and her meats and all the culinary scheming of her well washed hands. The husband was different. Roger had once cracked a dirty joke with him which made him laugh. Now he was always greeted with a wink and the shadow of an elbow nudge. The husband was debonair and more or less drunk most of the time. Nicely drunk, humanely drunk, definitely drunk. He was at the other end of the shop when Roger pushed open the door. He was talking to a man of the cloth, purple vested, white collared, well tailored suit, well oiled. A high class bishop on a Sunday holiday.

'Bless you my son,' the Bishop yelled from the bottom of the shop.

'Yes,' said Roger, looking here and there, hither and yon, hoping the Bishop was not addressing him and muttering

'Kabanos' at the low-browed lady through a frozen-toothed smile.

'A glass of wine,' yelled the drunken Bishop.

'Beef,' muttered Roger. The smile stuck to his dry teeth. The Italian lady's face gave him not a quiver of the moustachioed lip. The hand of God's representative on earth landed on Roger's shoulder, the beef slapped onto the glass top of the counter. Roger asked for two more kabanos but the hand remained, pressing his shoulder, giving him time to pay his money, gather his goods, lick his dry teeth before it pressed him down to the bottom of the shop and forced him into a bottle of wine.

'Wine,' said the Bishop.

'Communion,' said the delicatessen's husband.

'Thank you,' said Roger.

'Bless you,' said the Bishop.

'Thank you,' said Roger and they slugged the wine down in one, all three to a man, and stood in a half circle smiling Sunday morning smiles. The Bishop refilled the glasses.

'Communion,' he said.

'I've never been christened,' Roger said.

'Bless you,' said the Bishop.

'Thank you,' said Roger, drank down his wine, and left the shop with tears in his eyes, clutching kabanos and beef in his left armpit.

The adolescents were sitting on the benches. They didn't look at him. Bloody child. Bloody, bloody child. Tomorrow he'd appear in Churchillian rompers. Go to work in them. Storm the city. There was a pretty adolescent girl, flat chested and a sweatband round her young brown forehead, stork-legged, leaning against a wall. Walls were clean in Hampstead.

'Look at me,' he shouted, stuffing a kabanos in his mouth to stifle the scream and passing on. The summer breeze shifted his thin silk hair and he wanted to be beautiful.

Fuchsia had given Roger a toy for Christmas. Fuchsia was Roger's sister-in-law, Jade's sister, divorced with two King Charles spaniels, a very old Triumph Herald in excellent condition and heavy six foot by eight foot mirrors on the walls of her old town flat. Mirrors in golden frames.

Gilt. Fuchsia was a Dresden shepherdess and a devotee of Mervyn Peake. Her real name was Ann. Last Christmas Debenhams had a ridiculous sale and Fuchsia bought Roger a remote-controlled car. He had once played with it for a whole day. When he got back to the flat, he took it down from the top shelf of the glass-fronted oak bookcase, the only furniture in the small back room apart from a Habitat folding table and two large floor cushions covered in black Peter Jones cord, twelve pounds ninety-five a metre, never knowingly undersold. He took it down, dusted it, checked the batteries, put it back. He knew what boys liked. He gave the beef, the kabanos and the wine to Jade. He ran a hand over his hair and extracted three separate thinly shining threads. He ran his hand through again and got another four. He went to the bathroom and smiled at the mirror. Jade asked for the picnic hamper.

Three years ago, Christmas time, they had received a hamper from Fortnum's. Genuine basket, good sized, enclosing little jams and marmalade and teas, nuts and wine, pâté and anchovy paste, cranberry sauce and a Christmas pudding. Roger's firm was run by a man who was an expert in the art of debauch. Roger had hoped for better things. They kept the hamper under the divan, had never used it, always thought it would come in useful, a proper picnic hamper. Roger wanted to kiss Jade but she was cutting thin slices of delicate brown bread, had on her lipstick and would hate to be wet lipped by him when the air was blowing so fresh from the back balcony garden. Roger wanted to paint purple circles all over the misty beige walls but he didn't.

Underneath the five by six divan in the six by seven bedroom were four storage compartments. A clever arrangement. Roger could guarantee that anything he was looking for would be in the last compartment, even if he looked in the last compartment first which he always did. Roger wanted to run round the block but he knew he'd die after twenty yards. He'd contemplated it in moments of lighter depression as a possible means of suicide. He'd once seen a man dying of a heart attack. It wasn't pretty, definitely wasn't pretty, but it did the job. Underneath the payed for them with money from the pocket in the other leg of his combat trousers. The pocket he saved ten pees from the locker system in. Every time they went to the swimming pool he and the boy collected all the forgotten ten pees from the lockers. One of them stood look-out, the other did the deed. They regarded it not as stealing but as protective custody. It usually paid for their swim. The Muslim at the cash desk went on laughing.

'You go out?' he said.

'Picnic,' Naomi smiled at him. He sang her a strain of a Hindi love song but she didn't understand the words. John was out on the pavement so she blew the big Muslim a kiss.

'Have a very nice time,' he called and sang out louder as she left the shop. He was a very keen tennis player and had tried to join the local tennis club many times but they were full up and he was at the bottom of a very long waiting list. He'd asked her for a game once but she didn't have a tennis dress and was far too embarrassed to expose the whole length of her legs to him in cut-off jeans which folded into the bottom of her bum and rolled a little pocket of flesh out for all to see. Her bum, it had been said, was her best feature. It seemed to her obscene, trailing along behind her.

'Can I have a Coke at the railway station?' the boy said.

'Yes,' said Naomi.

'In a can?'

'Yes.'

'Why?'

'Special treat,' said Naomi. He was allowed Coke and sweets only on a Saturday.

'Think yourself lucky,' said John.

'Where do you find out how heavy whales are?' Naomi said it very slowly and carefully.

'I don't know,' said the boy.

'At a whale weigh station,' said Naomi. The boy laughed. John laughed too.

'Why did the dog cross the road?' said the boy.

'I don't know,' said Naomi.

'Because it wanted to go to the seaside,' said the boy.

The boy laughed. John and Naomi held hands and giggled with him. They passed the stripped pine shop with blow-brush pictures of knights errant in tones of sepia and watery green in the window.

'The guy who runs that place,' said Naomi, 'he's gay.'

'Which one?' said John.

'The one with the boots from Brixham,' said Naomi.

'Does it matter?'

'I thought he fancied me,' said Naomi, 'he used to smile at me.'

'You think everyone fancies you,' said John.

'The Scottish butcher did and the greengrocer,' Naomi said. 'The Scottish butcher leant over the counter, kissed me and gave me two pence off a pound of pork chipolatas and the greengrocer used to kiss my hand and tickle my ribs if he caught me alone in the baker's shop.'

'What about the baker?'

'She's a woman, thank God.'

'How do you know he's gay?'

'Doesn't matter, does it?'

'I'm curious.'

'You said it didn't matter.'

'For God's sake.'

'I saw him necking with a fella up the close next to the bookshop.'

'What did the fella look like?'

'Nice,' said Naomi.

They were at the railway station. John went to get the tickets. The ticket man slapped his change down onto the counter hard and glared at John. It was one of his two pleasures. He slapped the change down at the men so that they jumped, and folded it neatly into the women's hands so that they squirmed. Naomi unbuttoned the ten pee pocket on the leg of the combat trousers, pinched John's thigh, abstracted thirty pence and bought the boy a Coke.

'Thank you,' he said.

The train came immediately. The father chose the seats, the dark ones on the left at the front. The father always golf clubs in the third compartment Roger was panting but he found the picnic hamper. He dragged it out. Closed the lid. Replaced the mattress. Put back the pillows. Shook the duvet. Ran his hands over his hair. He got five hairs out and one silver. He never counted the silver. He took the hamper through to the bathroom, smiled at himself in the mirror. His face was grey white. There was sweat on his top lip. He put the hamper down and had a shit. Any physical exercise moved his bowels. Considering how much came out of him, it was amazing that he retained his fat baby body. He wiped his bottom carefully. Washed it with a sponge and cold water. Jade said cold water prevented haemorrhoids. He didn't want haemorrhoids. He pulled up his track-suit trousers. He smiled in the mirror purely for courage and took the hamper through to the back room. He turned the air conditioning on in the bathroom and stirred the pot pourri on the back room table. Roger was afraid of air conditioning. Legionnaires' disease haunted him. He had asked Jade to buy buckets of pot pourri. They might not be able to afford a larger Hampstead residence but they could afford buckets of pot pourri. So far she had bought one bowl. Sometimes Jade found it very difficult to leave the house. Roger's shit was particularly noxious and one could not greet one's friends with noxious odours pervading the atmosphere. Even if they did have a child.

Jade filled the hamper. Coffee freshly ground, brewed and flasked. Mugs, red plastic; plates, red plastic. Swedish knives and forks. Red plastic bowls of potato salad, tomato and cucumber, prawns, many, many prawns; daintily wrapped delicatessen meat and kabanos, bread, cake and wine; condiments, all packed in the Fortnum's Christmas hamper. Jade collected rugs and a white linen table cloth with matching napkins. Jade slipped into her thermal underwear. Jade did not trust summer. The picnic was ready. Jade rubbed Roger's temples. They had received a book on massage for the relief of pain. Roger was always more or less in pain because Roger was always more or less afraid. Jade fastened gold chains around her wrists and Roger slid a white opal ring onto her finger. He had given it to her when they first met. Then he'd worn black leather, had long flowing hair and ridden a motorbike. He sent a message to Jade saying she was the most beautiful woman he'd ever seen and would she go out with him. Jade sent a message: 'yes'. They met. He all in black leather, she all in green silk pyjamas and a wide hood on her head and he gave her the opal ring. Her nails were long and painted red. Her fingers were slender as an indolent emperor's. They fluttered when she spoke. Her hands were white. Opalescent. The ring had come from his great grandmother. They talked of her all evening. Jade believed in communing with spirits and took him next evening to a spiritualist circle where indeed his great grandmother communed through the ring and sent messages of bland hope.

The entryphone buzzed. 'Hello it's us' sounded through the summer flat. He hated that 'Hello it's us'. He hated the arrogance of it. Didn't want to go for a picnic. Wanted to stay here all day. Lie on the floor with the breeze blowing the curtains. Paint purple circles on the wall. Find the adolescent girl, leaning with the sweatband round her forehead. Wanted to. Wanted to. He ran his hand down the length of Jade's hair. Pushed the button which opened the door downstairs which let 'us' in.

'It was a full moon last night,' Naomi said.

'What's the weather forecast?' John turned up the volume on the radio.

'It's best under a full moon.' Naomi put her arms round John's neck and thrust herself up against him. He struggled with the volume button on the radio.

'God damn it,' he said, 'we've missed the weather forecast.'

'Let's go back to bed,' Naomi said, kissing at him, drawing his head down to her, kissing his mouth though he hated to be kissed.

'For God's sake, woman,' he said, 'get dressed.'

Naomi slid her arms off. 'I'm feeling randy,' she said. John kissed her cheek.

'Matthew,' John said, 'we're going out.' He pulled Matthew away from the boy's head and dislodged two pieces of track.

'I'll tell my mummy on you,' Matthew said and he fussed at the tracks.

'Thank you for having me,' said the boy.

'I'm going to have an ice cream with two chocolate flakes and raspberry sauce and chocolate sauce,' said Matthew, 'and you're not.'

'I'm going on a train,' said the boy and walked out of the house.

Thirty pence a pair, the old shoemaker at the bottom of the road sold white cotton shoelaces at, six feet long. They were kept locked in the dressing-table drawer to use as a special treat. Naomi threaded them into bright green boots. She liked herself in the mirror sloping against the wall. The boy threw himself through the door and jumped on the bed, trying to touch the ceiling. He thudded down on the bed springs and made the floor shake.

'It's a very old house,' she said.

'You look nice,' said the boy.

John ran up the stairs. 'For God's sake,' he said, 'take a sweatshirt. You'll freeze to death.'

'I can't wear a sweatshirt with this,' she said.

'Do what you like.' John thumped back downstairs, she heard him sit on the sofa. She heard the squeak of his teeth on the flesh of his thumb as he chewed at it like an old piece of rubber.

Naomi opened the drawer and took out a blue sweatshirt with a cut-off neck. She tucked it into the belt.

'Open the blind,' the boy said. She stood on the arm of the yellow armchair and tied the blind to a rusty nail at the top of the window frame. Across the road Max was sitting in his chair on the front doorstep prepared for the world to walk by. He had his stick beside him and a cup of tea, a bible in his hand. Naomi gave him a wave.

'Did he wave?' the boy said. 'Did he? Did he?'

'No,' said Naomi. 'He will one day. Come on,' she said, 'Daddy's waiting.'

The boy stopped jumping. 'Perhaps he's blind,' he said.

'Who?'

'Bill,' said the boy. 'Perhaps he can't see you waving.'

'He can see,' Naomi said. Bill spent every night peeping out from behind his curtain, looking straight through the bamboo blind at Naomi undressing.

'What do you think about a bright green duvet cover?' she asked the boy.

'Why?'

'Just for fun,' said Naomi.

'Stupid,' said the boy and thumped his mother hard on the backside.

When they got downstairs John had laid out rain things. They were laid out on the kitchen table and Naomi decided to ignore them. She picked up a book for the boy and put it into her shoulder-bag. She brushed the boy's hair. When he winced she said, 'If you don't like having it brushed I'll cut it off.' The boy was proud of his hair, which very nearly touched his shoulders.

'Ready,' she called through to John.

'Knickers,' he said and he put an arm round her shoulders.

Down at Baashi's they bought presents for Jade and Roger, an onion bhaji for Naomi and a packet of crisps for the boy.

'You never have anything,' Naomi said. 'Why can't you have little indulgences?' He was wearing his austere face and paying for the onion bhaji as a separate item with the loose change from the leg pocket in his combat trousers.

'We can't afford it,' he said. She took an overlarge mouthful of onion bhaji and chewed it at him. The big Muslim with the beard behind the counter laughed at her. She liked him. He liked her because she liked onion bhaji and didn't like samosa with meat and neither did he. The boy took a long time deciding which packet of crisps to have. He ended up with the ones he usually had and John

'We're going for a bloody picnic,' he said. 'Pull yourself together.'

She flung herself onto him, tied herself round his neck and twined round his legs. 'You don't think I'm sexy any more.'

John turned her round and slapped her bum hard. 'We're late,' he said. 'Get dressed.' The child rattled into the kitchen.

'Can I ride out?' he said. 'Matthew is on the pavement.'

'Five minutes,' said John. 'We're late.'

The child grabbed his bike, still with stabilizers on, crashed it into the woodwork round the back door, scraped some more paint off and bounced the bike out into the yard.

'A five-minute fuck,' Naomi said.

'If you want me to phone them up and tell them we're not coming, I will,' said John.

Naomi went upstairs and took off her dressing-gown. The room needed redecorating. The lampshade was covered in dust. Naomi hated dusting, John only did floors. The long mirror, gift of an old girlfriend of his, leant propped against the wall. It had been there, propped, for two months. Naomi lay naked full length on the bed and gazed into the corner where the wallpaper was coming off.

'We'll have to do something about this room,' she yelled down to John.

'Are you ready?' He was getting bad tempered.

'Nearly. I don't know what to put on.' She heard John gallop up the stairs. She leapt off the bed and wound her naked body round him.

'For God's sake,' he said. She put her hand on his penis. John dragged a skirt off the hatstand in the corner. He had to stretch out full stretch to do it. Naomi buried her mouth in his neck.

'Let's make a baby,' she said between mouthfuls of skin.

John tugged at the skirt, pulled at it, tugged at it, pulled the skirt off the hatstand and the hatstand down on top of them both. The brim of Naomi's hard hat which she had had since she was twelve dug John just above the left eyebrow. Naomi was buried in festooned lengths of old cotton skirts. She giggled and waited for John to join in. Nothing. She walked the hatstand back up into the corner. John's face had retired behind his eyebrows.

'If we bought a new duvet cover,' she said, 'bright green, that'd do something.' She flung a great blue skirt over her head and fastened it at the back. She opened a drawer and pulled on a lacy underskirt.

'Don't you think?' she said.

'Don't forget your knickers.' John was rubbing his head. His left eye was watering. 'That hatstand's a bloody stupid idea.' Naomi fastened on a lacy camisole, pulled a wide belt round her waist as tight as it would go and then tighter.

'You'll be cold,' John said.

'It is summer.' Naomi started to put on thick creamy tights.

'Knickers,' John said and left the room. Naomi sat down on the bed. She pulled her skirt right up.

'Never mind,' she told her deserted crutch and gave it a pat for good luck.

John yelled for the boy out the front door. There was no reply. He walked up the road. The bike was parked neatly outside Matthew's front window. He discovered his son a prisoner of Matthew's train set, in Matthew's front room, sitting in the middle of a great circle of track, allowed to look, not allowed to touch. Matthew was at the controls.

'Come on,' John said, 'we're late.'

'He can stay here,' Matthew said.

'We're going out,' said John.

'That's alright,' Matthew said, 'he can stay with us. I'll ask my Mummy.' And he put his hand very firmly on the boy's head. Matthew standing up, the boy kneeling in the circle of track. Matthew leaning very heavily on top of the boy's head so that he couldn't get up, pushing down so hard that the boy's teeth ground together and he couldn't speak. John leant into the middle of the magic circle and grabbed Matthew's arm.

'Don't stand on my track,' said Matthew. 'Don't stand on my track.'

hid on trains. The boy did not follow him. He sat in the sun and Naomi sat beside him. John moved to be with them.

'Did you see that bloke on the platform?' Naomi said.

'I'll have my Coke and crisps now. Open them.' The boy handed them to Naomi.

'Please,' said Naomi.

'Please,' said the boy.

'You open the Coke.' Naomi gave the can to John.

'Have you shaken this?' John said. The boy shook his head. Naomi handed him the open packet of crisps.

'Are you sure?' John cocked his head on one side and tested the boy for honesty. He opened the can.

'What bloke?' He gave the can to the boy.

'Put the crisps between your legs,' Naomi said. The boy smiled at her.

'Face like a girl,' she said to John. 'Pouting lips, curls, tall, delicately thin. Great shadows under his eyes.'

'How did you see all that?'

'He lives in our road, at the top. In the house with the trees in front of the windows. He's a debauched angel.'

'How do you know he's debauched?'

'All those leaves over his windows. Must be dark in there.'

'That doesn't make him debauched.'

'You don't know.'

'Neither do you.'

'He looks like a debauched angel.'

'That's better,' said John. 'He's an androgyne.'

'You saw him.'

'Of course I saw him.'

'How do you know he's an androgyne?'

'For God's sake, Naomi.'

'You fancy him.'

'You're the one who can describe him down to the colour of his eyes.'

'I like his flanks. I'm not bothered about the colour of his eyes.'

'What are flanks?' said the boy.

'The fleshy bit at the rear end of an animal or a human being,' John said.

'Bum,' said the boy. 'Human beings *are* animals,' said the boy.

'Who says?' said John.

'Mrs Grierson.'

'Mrs Grierson may be a very good teacher,' said John, 'but . . .'

'And Naomi,' said the boy and he crunched one of Britain's noisiest crisps.

'I thought he looked sinister,' said Naomi. 'I didn't fancy him.'

'Neither did I,' said John.

'Do you fancy the fella in the stripped pine shop?'

'No.'

'That's all right then,' said Naomi. 'Who do you fancy?'

'You,' said John.

'Can we make a baby tonight?'

John sighed and looked out the window.

'We are animals,' the boy said.

'I know that,' said John.

'Your father is the only man of his time and cultural background who actually believes in God and the soul,' said Naomi.

'Mrs Grierson says about Jesus,' said the boy.

'Well,' said Naomi, 'it's a nice story.'

'It's true,' said the boy. 'I like heaven.'

'I like earth,' said Naomi, 'it's a lot of fun.'

'I could have a BMX bike in heaven.'

'You can't even ride a bike without stabilizers.'

'I could in heaven.'

'And I could play the bagpipes,' said Naomi.

Big Ben floated up on the left hand side covered in polythene and scaffolding.

'And I could have Coke every day not just Saturdays and special treats.'

'You wouldn't want it,' said Naomi.

'Oh yes I would,' said the boy and he scrunched himself into the corner of his seat, creating as much space between himself and his mother as he could, so that no part of him touched any part of her.

'You don't know anything,' he said.

Naomi kissed the top of his head and put her arm round the boy's shoulder.

'I'm being silly,' she said.

The boy emptied the crisp crumbs into his mouth and snuggled into Naomi's side.

'Come on,' said John. The train had stopped.

'Can I have a croissant filled with cheese?' Naomi said. There was a patisserie on the way to the tube.

'Thirty-five pence for an onion bhaji, forty-five pence for a croissant,' John said.

'Please,' said Naomi. 'I'm hungry.'

'You'll get fat,' John said and he bought a cheese croissant from the girl in the pretty cap and apron behind the counter. He bought a spinach one for himself.

'I wish they did them with wholewheat flour,' said Naomi, pastry flakes falling from her mouth and down the front of her sweatshirt.

'I don't,' said John. 'It's a treat.'

'Will there be Coke at their house?' said the boy.

'Come on,' said John.

The escalator was broken so they walked down the stairs.

'I hope it's fixed on the way back,' Naomi said.

'Why?' said the boy.

'It's harder walking up than it is walking down.'

'Why?'

'You have to lift your own weight up each step.'

'Why?'

Naomi stuffed the end of her croissant into her mouth so that she couldn't answer.

There was a violinist in one tunnel, classical, a clarinettist in the second, jazz and an amplified acoustic guitar winging out Simon and Garfunkel in their tunnel. The man playing it had a three-day Yasser Arafat growth kept at three days with busy scissors to present a carelessness which did not exist, but he could sing. Naomi and the boy stopped opposite him and smiled. Naomi picked the boy up in her arms and the man smiled at them. John walked round the corner to the platform. The man was playing 'The Boxer'. Naomi and the boy joined in on the 'lie la lies'. At the end the man put his guitar down and walked across to them. He held ten pee out to Naomi.

'Thank you,' she said and took it. The man smiled at her.

'My mummy plays that song,' the boy said.

'Who's your mummy?' said the man.

'She is,' said the boy.

'Doesn't look old enough,' said the man. 'Does she play it better than me?'

'And sings better,' said the boy.

The man smiled at Naomi. He dug his hand into his other pocket, took out a wallet filled with notes.

'You've got a lot of money,' said the boy. The man handed Naomi a white oblong.

'My card,' he said. Naomi took it. 'You and I could make a fortune,' he said, 'if you ever want a job.'

Naomi smiled. She kept the card in her hand. She set the boy on his feet. They walked off down the tunnel hand in hand. Naomi waved the card in her hand high in the air.

'Think about it,' the man yelled down the tunnel.

'I will,' Naomi yelled back.

'We missed a train.' John's face was stern.

'There'll be another one.' Naomi linked her arm into his. 'Keep this for me,' she said.

'What is it?'

'I might need a job one day,' Naomi said. John drew apart from her. Naomi tucked the card into her belt.

'You're like a little child,' John said, 'drawing attention to yourself.'

'He could really sing,' Naomi said.

'Little girl. Always, always,' said John. 'Let's make a baby, onion bhajis. We can't afford a baby, we can't afford onion bhajis and we certainly can't afford cheese croissants.'

'You had a spinach one,' Naomi said.

'That was a mistake,' said John.

'Have you got indigestion?'

'No I have not.' John put his hand on his son's shoulder.

'You're an ordinary woman, Naomi. You've got grey hair. Grow up, will you.' Naomi turned away from him. 'You're the only person I know who seeks out encounters in tube stations.' The boy held tight to Naomi's hand. 'You'll get yourself into trouble,' John said. Naomi did not turn back. 'I worry about you.'

'If I took the job we could afford cheese croissants,' said Naomi.

'And a car,' said the boy.

'You see,' said John. 'Is this good for him? Is it?' When the tube came he let them take their seats. He walked down to the opposite end of the carriage and sat with his back to them.

'Why is he cross?' the boy said.

'Just is,' said Naomi. The boy reached up and touched her hair.

'I like your hair.'

'You once beat me up because of it,' Naomi said.

'When did I?'

'First time you noticed it was grey.'

'Was I a baby?'

'No,' said Naomi. 'We were sitting on the back grass. It was a hot day and we'd had a picnic, apples, cheese, bread and juice on the rug. Then we flopped out in the sun. You were pulling my face into Chinese eyes. All of a sudden you stopped. "What's that?" you said and you tugged at my hair. Then you started to cry and hit me at the same time.'

'Did it hurt?'

'Yes.'

'Were you cross?'

'No.'

'Couldn't have hurt then,' said the boy. 'I like it now.'

The tube stopped. A girl walked on and sat down opposite. Naomi stared. The boy stared. The girl had bright blue-black hair, her face was geisha painted. She had a black skirt slashed to the waist, laced up the side with thongs. The skirt was tight. Ruched under it, meant to be seen in the spaces between the thongs, was a white cotton underskirt. The skirt was so tight it forced the girl's knees together.

'Chastity belt,' thought Naomi.

'What?' said the boy. The girl had one bare shoulder. 'She looks nice,' said the boy and he didn't whisper. The girl smiled at him and her teeth were yellow against the white face.

'I think she's beautiful,' said the boy. The girl laughed at him and got off at the next stop.

'I wish you'd dress like that,' said the boy. 'Why don't you?'

'I wouldn't be able to run.'

'You could wear make-up,' said the boy.

'I wonder where she was going,' Naomi said.

'Fairyland,' said the boy, 'to meet the A-team.'

'Why?'

'I know she was,' said the boy. 'And she'd ride a bike.'

'They don't have bikes in fairyland.'

'They do,' said the boy, 'I know they do.'

'They don't,' said Naomi.

'They do,' said the boy. 'They do if I want them to.'

Naomi sulked. 'She wouldn't be able to ride a bike,' she said, 'because her skirt was too tight and she'd fall on her nose over the handlebars.'

'You,' said the boy, 'you don't know anything.' He looked at his father's back down at the other end of the carriage. It was stiff. He looked at Naomi.

'I knew it would be like this today,' he said. Naomi wiped the sulk off her face, put her arm round the boy's shoulders and laughed.

'Got a kiss?' she said.

'I ran out,' said the boy.

'I'd better give you one,' she said. 'Come close,' she said. 'Closer.' The boy reached his face up and Naomi kissed him.

'I would rather, you know, have played with Laurie.'

'It'll be fun,' said Naomi.

She looked down the carriage to John at the other end. He had found a Sunday magazine.

'I hope it's the *Observer*,' Naomi said.

'What?'

'Your father's found a Sunday paper. If it's the *Times* or

the *Telegraph* he'll be cross.' Sunday papers had been too expensive in their house since before Christmas.

'Why?' said the boy.

When they'd had them, Naomi who hated papers would be cross all day because John was reading them, laboriously, front to back, word for word and all the adverts. John would be cross because he never found what he wanted. Nothing was cheap enough to buy and none of the information was adequate.

'I don't know,' Naomi said.

'I clean the floors.' John held the *Observer* magazine nine inches from his nose so that other passengers on the Sunday tube might not be disturbed by the twitching of his face.

'I do the ironing. My son's best friend's mother called me domesticated and she didn't mean it kindly. Unmanly, that's me. I can run three miles without stopping. Run, not jog, run. Unmanly. A purple room. Big flat I shared before domestic bliss and I painted my room purple. Big, old flat. Do you hear me, Laurie's mother?'

John put his hand up to his eye. A pulse was beating in the under lid.

'That. That only happens when I'm tired. Tired out. Ironed for three hours yesterday. On my feet for three hours. Stamina. In my purple room I deflowered maidens. They queued up at my bloody door. Do you hear me, Laurie's mother? I was a stud. A kindly stud. Kindly John. Kindly, kindly stud John. The lampshade was purple. Painted that myself. Great paper lampshade. You couldn't buy purple paper lampshades. Took me hours to paint that so the paper didn't crack. Candlewick bedspread, bedsheets. Dyed. Dyed the carpet even. And I burned incense in my purple painted fireplace. Give me back my room. She, Naomi, Laurie's mother, your friend, damn it, Laurie's mother, she should behave when we come out.

'Domesticated.' John's face was still. He lowered the *Observer* magazine. Only his foot performed an unusual range of movements. He uncrossed his legs. He placed his foot firmly on the floor, sole to heel, flat down, side by side with the other one.

'Laurie's mother. We are neither of us domesticated. Both of us hate housework passionately. If we had money we would employ some little woman, release some woman from the prison of her house into the prison of ours. We would provide employment for small-time decorators, rubbers down of rusted guttering, painters of rotting window frames. We would feed them cups of tea and bought organic biscuits and talk to them as we would to equals. We have no money, Laurie's mother, and so we respect each other's hatred and share. We are vagabonds, Laurie's mother. Gypsies with a desire for order.

'The girls used to have me, not I them. My reputation spread by word of mouth. I was gentle, considerate and I never told, they did the telling. I liked girls. Still do. Never frightened one in my life. I felt sorry for them so I did what I could. "George's". George was a Hungarian. It always followed the same pattern. They'd invite me to George's for a meal. Company and a chat. They'd talk about D. H. Lawrence, surprising number of them. We'd split the bill. I ate lightly for the work ahead. They stuffed their faces out of fear. We'd linger outside supposedly saying goodnight, then a hand would creep into mine and off we'd go.

'"My husband," you say, Laurie's mother, "my husband may have faults but he's out in the world. Adventuring. Never washed a floor in his life. I do all the decorating, mend the washing machine, fix the plumbing, shop, clean, cook, look after the child and lie frigid in bed."

'There was a service I had to perform. Listen to me, Laurie's mother. In my purple room I gently deflowered maidens. I had an old Cannon gas fire, heavy black metal thing. I lit candles and I made love on the purple rug. At the end of four years I took my 2.2 and moved as far from that place as I could go. Get your comfort where you can, Laurie's mother, get your comfort where you can.'

John looked in to the dark tunnel and gathered himself bunched tight for a day of conquest to take home to Laurie's mother and lay at her feet.

* * *

'It is autumn,' thought Naomi. 'I am Sarah Jane, curly hair pulled back, tendrils escaping wild, black eyes flashing under demure lids, russet apple cheeks. I am a serving maid. In my lap a black silk shawl festooned with roses. I put tassels on the shawl, long trailing, thin dangling. Run them through your hands for the kiss of the silk. A falling leaf tickle. Outside, a pregnant moon. Like me, full of fruit and happy as a chuckle. I sit in a grandmother chair on blue cotton cushions cheery bright, left over from the curtains. Curtains generous enough to pull and fall in great folds across the window, keep out the draughts, keep out the dark. I haven't pulled them tonight. I'm sitting by my great hearth fire. I'm letting the moon in. Full bellied, big bosomed, she's coming in for supper.'

'Which side will it be?' said the boy.

'That one.' Naomi pointed to her left.

'That one.' The boy pointed to his right. The tube pulled in to the platform on the right. 'I won, I won,' said the boy.

'For God's sake.' John's voice swooped down the carriage at them. He was holding the door at his end. They were supposed to be getting off.

'Are we here?' said the boy.

The doors had opened and shut. John still held his open. Manfully.

'Hurry,' Naomi said. She dragged the boy towards the open door.

'Why?' he said.

'Off,' she said and they both jumped through the space, missed the gap and landed on the platform.

'For God's sake,' John said.

The guard took long enough to glare before sending the train on its way. Naomi stared at her boots. The boy hid in her skirt. John burst into great guffaws of laughter so that the tube tunnel echoed.

'Daddy.' The boy smiled and played at being a dog, whined and pawed at the waist of his father's combat trousers. John picked him up.

'This has been a ridiculous morning.' He let Naomi sidle

into him.

Up in the air after the lift, a search for tickets and a demand for chocolate, the wind and the blue sky made the boy laugh.

'I'm glad I wore a sweatshirt,' Naomi said.

'You are a twit,' said John.

'I earned more than you last year,' said Naomi.

'Not if you count my dole.'

'You can't count dole.'

'It's taxed,' said John.

'I still earned more than you.'

'I'll crack it next year,' said John. 'Next year,' said John, 'we'll buy a house with a study.'

'And an extra bedroom,' said Naomi, 'for the baby.'

'If I crack it you can have triplets.'

'That fruit shop's got mangoes on a Sunday and they're a pound each,' said Naomi. John put the boy down. He went into the shop.

'Don't, John,' said Naomi. When he came out he was carrying a mango, green and red blush. He sat on a bench.

'We should be there by now,' Naomi said. She and the boy sat down beside him and watched. John took out his Swiss army knife. He'd found it in the gutter three years ago, outside their front gate, presented it to the police and got it back six months later. Something for nothing. An honest knife. It was his most prized possession. He sliced the mango with the Swiss army knife, dug out the stone and gave it to the boy to put in the litter bin at the side of the bench.

'What will it taste like?' said the boy.

John handed him a slice. The boy held it in his hand. John gave Naomi the second slice. She held it waiting for him. Their first fresh pineapple they'd shared at their first love-making. In front of an electric fire, three bars full on, eating slices off each other's bare bellies.

'I've never tasted mango,' she said.

'I was once sent a case,' he said, 'all the way from India. A dozen mangoes,' he said, 'and I had to pay twelve pounds duty.'

'Who sent them?' said Naomi.

'I ate them,' he said, 'all by myself. Ready?' he said.
'Who?' said Naomi.
He slivered a sliver of mango into his mouth.
'There,' he said with splurts of juice dribbling at the corners.
A little girl, at least three, dressed in calf-length trousers striped red and white, with a matching sweatshirt, stood at the end of the bench staring at them. Her hair was tied with red and white ribbons in six pigtails.
'She's got six pigtails,' said the boy and he stared at her.
'You haven't tasted your mango,' John said.
'Can I give it to her?' said the boy.
He held the mango out to the little girl in a sweaty hand covered in a mist of grub. She took it and smiled, stuffed it into her mouth and the juice trickled down the front of her red and white sweatshirt. She wiped her hands on her cotton trousers and her mouth on her sleeve.
'Now you,' John said.
He gave the boy another piece of mango. The boy shoved it into his mouth, chewed and swallowed as fast as he could.
'Naomi hasn't tasted hers,' said the boy.
'More,' said the little girl. Her mother, dressed all in white with very long legs, took her sticky hand and pulled her away.
'Right,' said Naomi. She dropped the piece of mango into her mouth and chewed.
'Well?' said John.
'You can finish it,' said Naomi. John held a piece out to the boy.
'That's all right, you have it, Daddy.'
'I will,' said John. He ate it tidily, dabbed at his mouth with a handkerchief.
'We ought to get on,' Naomi said.
John wiped his hands on the handkerchief and buttoned it into his loin pocket.
'Right,' he said.
'I like peaches and raspberries and apples and bananas,' said the boy.

'Strawberries,' said Naomi.
'Strawberries,' said the boy.
'Come on,' said John.

Naomi gazed into the windows of the boutiques as they passed. Nothing had a price on. She wanted to see the reflection of a girl in an Indian dress and bare feet, wearing bells, but it was herself she saw, grey hair and beloved child in hand. She pointed to a bright white camisole with an edging of creamy lace and pearl buttons down the back. It was silk.

'That's beautiful,' she said.

'Not as nice as the ones you make,' said John.

'You can't wear white, not all white, unless you've got a nanny and your own car,' said Naomi. 'You can't wear white on a tube train.'

'You'd look nice all in white,' said John.

'The whole thing's stupid,' said Naomi.

'Do we go down here?' said John.

'You know as well as I do.'

'Why are you cross?' said the boy.

'A pound for a bloody mango,' said Naomi.

'Is it down here?' John said.

'Rings on my fingers and bells on my toes and silk on my back,' said Naomi, 'That's what I want. Not bloody mangoes.' John put his arm round her shoulders.

'A house with a study,' he said. Naomi shrugged away from his arm and knelt down beside the boy.

'I used to have silver rings for every finger,' she said. 'More than one on some. I even had rings on my thumbs. One was a woman's face, cross-looking, like a silver cameo, one was a flower, all its petals in silver. I had silver chains on my wrists and a great heavy arm band round the top of my arm with carbuncles of coral set into it. When we sold it we discovered it was very old indeed. Roman. We got a lot of money for it.'

'Did you sell all of it?' said the boy.

'I even had a thick linked silver ankle bracelet like chain mail with tiny silver bells attached.'

'Where's the money?' said the boy.

'Next year we'll crack it,' said John.

'We ate the money long ago,' said Naomi. 'I don't really want it, not any of it.' She looked at John. 'Coming here . . .'

'Is it down this way?' John held out his hand.

'It's silly not to be able to afford a baby.'

They walked past opulence and umbrellas on the pavement.

'Which one is it?' John said.

'She said they'd had it painted and a great storm had washed half the paint off the front of the house onto the pavement.'

'This is it,' John said. They walked up the steps to the front.

'Sodding entryphones,' John said. He pressed the buzzer. 'Are you going to speak or am I?'

'You,' said Naomi.

'It's us,' John said into the speaker, mouth close to it, posh voice on.

The small voice came up the stairs all the way from the bottom to the top. It had never encountered an entryphone. Roger was shaking. The small voice was on the first landing. There was sweat on Roger's brow. Jade gripped his hand and moved a black Chinese cup from the dining-table to a high shelf. It was three hundred years old. They drank herb tea from it, turn and turn about, for fun. Jade greeted the child in the hall outside the front door of the flat. She called the child 'darling' and the little voice was silenced.

Roger was alone in the back room. Panic beat at his heart and his temples. He was going to have a stroke. A man at work knew a man who knew a man who'd had a stroke just the other day, at thirty-three. Roger was going to die all alone in the back room. Beating. Beating. He felt sick. Sweat oozed down from his buttocks. The soft grey velour track-suit bottom caught it and held it. It would look like shading, the wetness. It trickled down past the backs of his knees.

The child burst into the room and stood stock still. They

stared at each other, Roger and he. The child's face was grave. The child's eyes were dark and patient.

'People who haven't got children never have toys,' he said.

'I have,' said Roger.

'Have you?' said the child. 'I've got lots of toys. What have you got?'

'Not lots,' said Roger. He felt proud because his toy was a goody. He knew the boy would like it. He was still sweating. He wanted to tease the moment out.

'You're very hot,' said the child.

Roger licked the sweat from his top lip. It tasted of ammonia. It tasted sick.

'Are you a man?' said the child.

Roger put his hand up to his hair. Four came away. The child's father was standing in the doorway. Short hair, short thick hair.

'You find it,' said Roger.

'What?' said the child.

'The toy,' said Roger.

'I don't know what it is,' said the child.

'You'll know when you see it,' said Roger.

'Sometimes I'm not very good at finding things,' said the child. And he took his eyes away and walked on into the room. And Roger wanted him still to stand there. He wanted the child to protect him from the man with the full head of short hair and the body, broad shouldered, standing in the doorway. His friend.

'John.' He held out his hand and saw a bead of sweat roll down the life line.

'Summer's come,' he said to excuse the damp heat of his handshake. 'So good to see you.' He smiled mentally at himself in the mirror.

The big slender man strode into the room and the summer shone in his eyes and his hair. Still eyes. He took Roger's hand and said he was looking well.

'I haven't found it yet,' said the boy. It was above his head.

'You're close,' said Roger.

He desperately wanted the boy to find it. Now. Before

the women came into the room. Naomi and Jade.

'You're very hot,' said Roger.

'Is it on the floor?' said the boy.

'No,' said Roger.

'Is it on the ceiling?' said the boy.

'No,' said Roger.

'Do you really want me to play with it?' said the boy

'Yes,' said Roger.

'Really?' said the boy.

'Yes,' said Roger.

'Why do you?' said the boy.

'Toys need to be played with,' said Roger and he smiled at John.

'You don't play with it,' said the boy.

'No,' said Roger.

'Where is it?' said the boy.

'Here,' said Roger and he took the car from the shelf, with the controls, put the car on the floor and the controls into the boy's hand. It was a big car, it was shiny, it was old fashioned and it was red. The boy and Roger were delighted. The car stilled the beating of Roger's heart and the boy's liking took the pain from his head.

'Someone's alive in here,' spoke Roger's mind. 'Someone's alive in here.' He didn't look at John.

Naomi was chattering. It had occurred to Jade many times in the past that if she wasn't Jade, she'd like to be Naomi. Of course Naomi wasn't beautiful, she wasn't clever, she wasn't stupid, she wasn't fat and she wasn't thin. There were many things Naomi wasn't and that was the beauty of her. She walked into the back room, chattering. She shoved a hand through her hair. Whipped a bag from her shoulder and rooted among the contents.

'We brought spices rare, a bottle of Martini and a jar of pickle. It's Mr Smith's Indian pickle made of cabbage and it comes from Tadcaster. Tadcaster's outside York,' she threw at Roger. 'What have you given him?'.

'You shouldn't have,' muttered Jade, gathering up the chana dall and fenugreek. She knew Naomi was poor. John was poor.

'Not at all,' said Naomi. 'I'd have bought a pineapple but I couldn't find one. I've always wanted to buy someone a pineapple. Roger, what have you given him?' She touched a light, light hand on her son's curly head. The boy looked up and grinned.

Roger plunged in misery. 'I haven't. Not given. I'm sure he . . .'

'Lended,' said the boy and took hold of Roger's sweaty hand.

'Lent,' said John.

'Lent,' said the boy.

'I've never tried one,' said Naomi. 'Can I have a go?'

'No,' said the boy.

'Please,' said Naomi.

'No,' said the boy. 'I'm going to play with it now, you can watch.'

Naomi saw the hamper. 'Jade, a real picnic hamper. I've always wanted one of those. You have such style.'

Jade smiled. 'I'm glad you think that,' she said.

'When I go for a picnic I'm lucky if I remember the sandwiches,' said Naomi.

'No sandwiches, I promise,' said Jade. 'Come and see the garden.' She led the way to the balcony, through the kitchen, just six feet outside the back room.

The boy was totally silent operating the controls of the red car. The men were totally silent watching him.

Naomi pointed to the red plastic plates and bowls in the white kitchen.

'You have style,' she said. She opened a tall three-cornered cupboard on the left of the balcony doors. Everything for the kitchen was in it, the rest was hanging on hooks.

'Everything red on hooks,' said Jade. She laid her hand

on a red plastic mug, extended her finger and pushed it so that it swung. She rattled her fingernails on a red plastic milk jug.

'This cupboard's brilliant,' said Naomi.

Jade smiled. The three-cornered cupboard was her own conception.

'We bought a freezer,' she said. 'I keep only prawns in it,' she said. And licked her glossed lips to make them shine.

'Where's the washing machine?' said Naomi.

'No room for both,' said Jade.

'Both what?' said Naomi, lost in the utter mundanity of the conversation, and Jade's eternal smile. She felt dull.

'Freezer and washing machine,' said Jade and went on smiling.

'Do you go to the launderette?' said Naomi.

'No,' said Jade.

'You wash by hand?' said Naomi.

'Yes,' said Jade. 'In the bath.' She let her mouth stretch into a fuller smile. She didn't believe in grins but the full smile, full and womanly.

'I couldn't,' said Naomi.

'Launderettes are depressing places,' said Jade. Naomi looked at her.

'You have to rub the collars of shirts, don't you? Once you start that you might as well keep going.'

'I don't,' said Naomi.

'What?'

'I don't rub the collars of shirts.' She looked into Jade's shining, womanly smile and waited for punishment to be meted out to her.

'Come into the garden,' said Jade.

They walked the four feet onto the balcony.

'Sometimes the towels build up,' said Jade. 'If someone's been staying the towels build up.' She sighed a hygienic housewife's stoic sigh. 'I find wringing them out quite tiring.'

'This is beautiful,' said Naomi standing on the balcony looking past the plants out at the trees and the other gardens. She listened to the silence between the men in the back room and calculated John's bad temper.

'What's that?' said Naomi. There was building going on, square little flats in pretty brick.

'Apartments,' said Jade. 'We looked at them. They're very small and one hundred and twenty thousand pounds. We decided that if we couldn't have exactly what we wanted we'd stay here.'

'You're very wise,' said Naomi. She worried about the silence between the men in the back room. Jade pointed at a tall tree. Her smile snapped out.

'I've always been afraid of that,' she said.

'Why?' said Naomi.

'If it falls,' said Jade.

'Ah,' said Naomi.

'It's very tall,' said Jade.

'It's beautiful,' said Naomi.

'I've no idea what it is,' said Jade. 'I lost all the geraniums from last year.'

'The pots are lovely,' said Naomi. 'Oh God,' thought Naomi.

'There's room for just two chairs. Would you like coffee?' said Jade. 'It's freshly brewed.'

'Please,' said Naomi. She sighed a small sigh. John liked coffee.

Jade went back to the kitchen and fiddled with some gadgets, displaying their glittery electric cleanliness with her perfect hands. She set a tray with tall coffee cups in thin grey china. The tray was black. She put out demerara sugar lumps with tongs in a matching grey bowl. She put the milk in a black jug. It was powdered and skimmed. She never used the stuff that looked as though it came from cows' insides.

'Your herbs are doing well,' said Naomi. She breathed in the coffee smell and tested the aroma on the tip of her tongue. John would like it. John would approve. John would be pleased and perhaps smile.

'I can't grow thyme,' said Jade.

'How do you manage to cook on a Baby Belling?' Naomi had a silent go at Fate and John for her service at the gates of Tesco's Instant Coffee's special hell.

'We have to make choices,' said Jade. 'I'm very proud that I've never bought a wok.'

'But you eat Chinese food all the time.' The smell must have reached John in the back room.

'A wok wouldn't fit on the cooker,' said Jade.

Jade looked at Naomi. She knew what she was doing. She watched Naomi throwing away the freezer and buying a full sized fridge. She watched her throw out the Baby Belling for a full sized cooker. Watched her cut out half the cupboard for a washing machine.

Jade took the tray through to the back room and put it on a black Habitat trolley pulled out from under the folding Habitat table. The men were silent, the child absorbed. She saw him spot the sugar lumps. They looked like the best kind of fudge. She saw him hesitate in his game. She placed a bowl of sugared almonds beside the sugar lumps. She wondered how long it would be before the child asked to eat the sugar lumps. She hoped she'd say yes.

'Do you eat much yoghurt?' Jade asked Naomi as she poured the coffee and passed it round.

'What can I drink?' said the child to no one in particular.

'Yes we do,' said Naomi, watching, watching John.

'I don't,' said the child.

'You do,' said Naomi.

'You can drink mineral water,' said Jade. 'Would you like some?'

'Yes,' said the child.

'Please,' said Naomi. She had helpless eyes on John.

'Please,' said the child.

Jade went into the kitchen. She poured Buxton water into a red plastic beaker.

'I make my own,' said Naomi. 'He won't eat it.' She threw her voice six feet into the kitchen. 'He eats natural yoghurt, always has, but you don't eat mine, do you?'

Jade brought the Buxton water into the back room. She

gave it to the child.

'Thank you,' said the child. Jade looked at him. He was beautiful.

'Pleasure,' she said.

The men were very quiet.

'How do you make it?' she said to Naomi. 'The yoghurt?'

The child sipped the mineral water. Jade wanted to string his curls through her fingers.

'It's fizzy,' he said. 'It doesn't taste,' he said, 'but it's fizzy.'

'Do you like it?' said Jade.

'Fucking come here,' thought John.

'Why don't you eat some sugar lumps?' said Jade. She handed him the bowl.

'Fucking two hours' journey. Costs a fucking fortune,' thought John.

'Oh God,' thought Naomi, hopeless eyes on John's face.

'Are they nice?' said the child.

'Why don't you try them and see?' said Jade. 'These are sugared almonds. You may taste these too.'

'Fucking inane, fucking conversation,' thought John. The child looked at his mother. Naomi nodded. The child put down his mineral water, carefully, on the floor. He took the two little bowls, one in each hand. He placed them beside the mineral water.

'Fucking red shiny face,' thought John of his friend Roger.

'Don't spill anything,' said Jade. She liked the child.

'Fucking red shiny fucking face,' thought John, staring at his friend Roger.

'I use a flask,' said Naomi.

'What for?' said Jade.

'Yoghurt,' said Naomi. 'I take a spoonful of the natural stuff and I heat milk, skimmed of course, and I pour the milk into the flask and leave it.'

Roger leant forward. His legs were slightly apart. He clasped his hands over the space between his thighs so that the sweat would run from his hands onto the carpet and not onto his track suit which was beginning to chafe his delicate skin it had become so wet.

'If they'd stop talking,' Roger thought.

'Would you like some culture?' said Jade.

'Sorry,' said Naomi.

'Let them stop talking,' Roger thought and he smiled at his friend John.

'A lady I work with gave me some culture,' said Jade.

'John,' said Naomi. 'Jade's got a beast.'

John looked at Jade. Jade cast her eyes down.

'Why do you call it a beast?' said Jade.

'It's alive, isn't it?' said Naomi. 'It grows.'

'This one's frozen,' said Jade.

'God, I'll believe in you if you'll stop them talking.' Roger cast his prayer out through the billowing net of the summer flat and rubbed his mental hands dry on his fat velour chest.

'It's supposed to last for a year frozen,' said Jade. 'We don't eat much yoghurt. It might be dead. You can have it if you want.'

'I'd love it,' said Naomi.

Roger felt a faint movement in his gut. Wind.

'I find it rather bitter,' said Jade.

'I like bitter yoghurt,' said Naomi.

'I don't,' said the child.

The wind moved gustily along Roger's intestinal tract. It hurt. Roger tensed his tubes against the pain.

'I can get some more,' said Jade, 'if it's dead.' There was a movement all along the lower half of Roger's belly as it pushed the wind along and down. Roger knew there could be only one possible result. He tensed his buttocks mightily and prayed.

The child began to guide the red car in and out of the coffee cups. He wasn't very good at it.

'Shall we go?' said Jade. She didn't want the child to do anything she would have to dislike him for. 'Put the car on the shelf. You can play with it when we come back.'

The child obeyed her instantly.

Roger felt the strain of his tight backside charge his retina with streaks of light. The company stood up.

'Do you like Jade's hair?' said Naomi.

'Yes,' said the child. He was looking at Jade's painted fingernails. She put the cups back on the tray.

'Where did it come from?' said Naomi.

Roger picked up the hamper. The lump of foul air had reached his rectum. He smiled at John with staring eyes, praying. John took the rugs. Naomi lifted the boy easily into her arms though he was nearly five.

'Russia,' said Jade.

'What kind of car have you got?' said the boy to Roger. Roger glowed under the direct beam of the boy's attention. The sweat came out on his top lip, his hands trembled, and he farted long and silently.

There was a huge silence in the room. Sulphur and corruption permeated the summer flat. Methane assaulted the revellers. There was a pause. Then Roger hummed a little Brahms. The fart lingered in the curtains, in the carpet, in the black cord fabric of the cushions.

'Pooh,' said the boy. 'Was that you, Nai?'

'Yes,' said Naomi. Roger was bright red. He avoided Jade's eyeline.

'John does stinkers,' said the boy.

'So do you,' said John.

'Not like yours,' said the boy. 'John's the champion.'

Roger stopped humming Brahms. He looked at the boy. He felt better.

'I've got a BMW,' he said.

The boy was quiet. He was still and he looked at Roger. Then, 'I think those are the very best cars,' he said.

Roger smiled at the boy. Jade smiled at Roger. Naomi and John smiled at each other.

The boy wasn't a very special boy, just an ordinary one. Once when asked what he wanted to be when he grew up, he smiled at his slightly arty parents and said, 'An ordinary man.' And his slightly arty parents had smiled at each other and the boy and his mother had gone off jogging round the block because they both had trainers. John and Naomi loved their ordinary boy very much and he loved them almost as much as he loved his best friend who lived across the road. He was stunningly beautiful, this ordinary boy.

* * *

The BMW was grey. The boy treated it with great respect. He laid his hand gently on the wing and stroked the metal.

'It's warm,' he said.

'That's the sun,' said Roger.

'You must be very rich,' said the boy.

'No,' said Roger. 'The people I work for gave me this.'

'That was very nice of them,' said the boy. 'My Daddy's on the dole.'

'Do you want to open the boot?' said Roger.

They opened the boot together, the boy and Roger. The hamper, the rugs and the linen table-cloth went in. Naomi stroked the hamper.

'I love baskets,' she said.

Roger asked the boy if he wanted to sit in the front seat with him. The boy told Roger it was against the law and put out his hand to touch Roger when he saw him blush and the sweat come out on his top lip.

'Naomi. I want you to sit beside me,' said the boy. It was hot in the car. They opened the windows. The Sunday shuffle sighed in at them. Hundreds of feet promenading.

'It's a lovely place to live,' said Naomi.

'We like it,' said Jade.

The boy was utterly silent. Utterly contented.

'We nearly phoned you last night to put this off,' said Naomi. 'The weather's been so dreadful.'

'We could have had it on the floor,' said Jade. They drove past Laura Ashley on one side and the Body Shop on the other. Naomi was faintly jealous. She made special trips to the Body Shop.

'Fancy having that at the top of your road,' she said.

'There was a report on face creams,' Jade said. She put a long white finger on her silky cheek and stroked it, little motions, going round. 'They looked at them all. Something wildly expensive came out top but not too top.' The white finger stroked and stroked.

'Before you say anything,' said Naomi, 'I use Jojoba from the Body Shop.'

Jade looked at Naomi's textured face. The white finger paused.

'That came out second,' she said. 'I use it myself.'

Naomi looked at Jade's skin. She tried to see lines round the eyes. There were none. She tried to see lines on the forehead. Jade turned to look through the windscreen. She put her beautiful hand on the back of Roger's neck. John stared at the hand stroking Roger's poor hair.

'That's nice,' Roger said.

'That's where the rich live,' Jade said, pointing to some hedges topped with burglar alarms. 'A sheikh bought one of the houses there, next door to his own. He knocked it down and built a squash court.'

Naomi thought sheikhs and squash were incongruous. She was unhappy. She couldn't take her eyes off her stubby brown hands. She watched John looking at Jade.

'You've had that ring a long time,' said John to Jade.

'You're saying let me kiss your hand,' thought Naomi.

'It's beautiful,' said John.

'Say what you mean,' thought Naomi. 'You're beautiful, you're beautiful let me touch your body.' She put her hand up to the grey streak at her right temple.

'Naomi,' said the boy.

'What?' said the woman. She put her hand on his shoulder. He looked out the window.

'Are we nearly there?' he said.

Roger glanced over his shoulder. 'Nearly,' he said.

'Do you remember, Roger?' said Naomi. 'Do you remember asking me to take a message to Jade before you had ever spoken to her. You said, "Will you tell Jade I think she is the most beautiful girl I've ever seen." Do you remember? "Will you ask her to meet me." And I did and you've been together ever since.'

'Don't go back that far,' said Jade.

'I remember when you screamed out "Knickers" at school and I was terribly shocked. You were wearing tartan Bermuda shorts and a red jumper and it was the middle of winter and I could never figure out why you weren't wearing school uniform.'

'Don't,' said Jade.

'Are we nearly there?' said the boy.

'Nearly,' said Roger.

'Why won't you look at me?' thought Naomi at John.

'This really is the best car,' said the boy.

'I've gone past it,' said Roger.

'Well just turn round and go back,' said Jade. She waved her hand in the air. The gold chains clinked. John was still watching.

'Look at me. Look at me,' thought Naomi.

'You've got a lot of gold on,' said the boy.

'I like it,' said Jade.

'So do I,' said the boy.

Naomi put her hand up to the silver chain round her neck. John had given her a present of a chain and an amethyst many years ago, in his purple period. The amethyst had disappeared.

'I like silver too,' said the boy.

'The gold glows on your skin,' said John, 'and picks up the lights in your hair.'

Roger jammed his angry grey machine to a juddering, crouching, waiting stance amidst the frolicsome lanes of Sunday drivers. The boy breathed out in delight.

'Hang on tight,' Roger yelled, 'we're going through.' He flung John hard against his seat belt. Naomi held the boy to her. Jade broke a nail against the front seat.

The grey car stroked its way through into the opposing stream of traffic.

'There,' said Roger. He dodged round a Ford Escort and smiled sweatily at the boy in the rear-view mirror.

'We're going to drive past the gates,' said Jade. 'Park here. Park here.'

'We could park inside,' said Roger.

'No, no, no,' said Jade. 'It'll be packed.'

Roger stopped parallel to Jade's indicated space. He calculated it was six inches larger than the car. Fourteen point four centimetres. One thousand four hundred and four millimetres. Roger set his charger prancing to the task. His cool hands grasped the controls of his great grey steed. The sweat of concentration stood out upon his manly brow. He calculated the angle nicely and with a prancing, sliding sidestep manoeuvred the great beast to its rest. Roger was panting, his hands stiff on the wheel, but he did not forget the pat of praise on the dashboard.

'I suppose,' said the boy, 'it would be easier to park a Mini.'

'A Triumph used to have a wonderful lock,' said Naomi. 'Does Fuchsia still have hers?'

'Yes,' said Jade.

'John,' said Naomi.

'What?' said John but he didn't turn his head.

'Look at me. Look at me,' thought Naomi. 'Nothing,' she said.

'What?' said John.

'I've forgotten what I was going to say,' said Naomi. She smoothed down her skirt. She tied her bootlaces. She smoothed her hair. She wiped a hand down over her face to rub it out but it wouldn't rub.

'It is winter,' thought Naomi, 'I am Sarah Lise, all cold as ice. Warm my feet, won't you hold my hand. Sarah never been loved Lise. Dwelling in a dark little hell hole, damp, up three flights facing the north wind. I clean the school of an afternoon and sit by a radiator smoking my last fag, running out of matches. I phone the council daily to fix my water, my sink, my heat, but they don't come and now I don't expect, feel grateful for the roof, the drying area, the neighbours knocking to see if I'm all right. I once was in love. Took me up a back close. Rammed into me, stuffed three quid into my hand and I ran all the way home with blood down my legs. The council came quick for the child out of that. I look out the window through the net and I spit at the grey sky, and I spit at the white ground and I rub my hands at the thin trees.'

'Naomi?' said the boy.

'What?' said Naomi. They were all outside the car looking at her.

'Come on,' said the boy.

'Sorry,' she said. The lace of her underskirt caught on the hook of her boot.

'Come on,' said John.

They already had the picnic out of the boot. Naomi bent over, one leg out of the car, tugging at the lace. Her face was red. Her grey and brown curls flopped forward onto her cheeks. Her skirt was thrown back and her pale tights gleamed into the boots.

'She looks like a milk flake ad,' said Jade.

'Let me,' said Roger. He bent down and quickly unhooked the lace. A worm was waking up in his brain. A silk worm. He gave Naomi his hand.

'You look very pretty,' he said and the sweat came out on his top lip. He was embarrassed.

'I feel tousled inside and out,' said Naomi.

'Oh, that was always your charm,' said Jade.

'Aren't you going to lock the car?' said the boy.

Roger patted his head and the boy let him. They locked the car together. John took the hamper in one hand and patted Naomi's hand with the other.

'Working-class winter,' thought Naomi, 'that's a bloody cheat. Let the summer be working class. Old people on a charabanc blaring Max Bygraves through the speakers and drowning him out with their out-of-time tuneless enjoyment. Stopping for a cup of tea and a bag of chips. Laughing and joking and talking about Bingo next Tuesday down the social. Long-faced boat trip, sightseeing round the Inns of Court, laughing at the men in wigs, that people should lead such a life. Doorstep sitting, fence leaning, tongue wagging, dinners cooking, extra portion for old Annie down the road what can't manage any more and doesn't want the meals strangers coming into her house. Labour Party posters in every window and a blessing on canvasser and candidate alike. Pounds for charity, pounds for Christmas Clubs, pounds for miners. "If we have to scrape a little it won't be what they have to do. Bless them. 'Course I don't hold with violence. Have another pound. Seems to me they're only hitting back with their fists what they're getting from them truncheons. Give us a badge. Our Jason collects badges. What do you want for that? Don't you give nothing away. You have another fifty pence and good luck to you I say. My Reg was redundant. Took him a good year to get work and he had qualifications. Sent him grey. You come back here another day. Day after tomorrow's insurance. I'll collect round the family, see what we can do. You come back Saturday. At the least we'll have tins for you, some of them nappies, disposable. We'll see what we can do. You come back Saturday, we'll clear out cupboards for you. Bless you, love, bless you."

'But I am Sarah Lise,' thought Naomi, 'and I still get cold in the winter time and had my babe to a man with tattoos on his arm who fucked me rigid up against a wall and gived me three nicker for me trouble and never knowed I loved him.'

'John,' said Naomi.

John kissed the top of her head.

'Look at me. Look at me,' thought Naomi.

John was watching Jade's bum wandering ahead of him. The boy took Naomi's free hand and bore down on it in excitement. They went through the gates.

'It said "out" there,' said the boy.

'Yes,' said Naomi.

'Why did we come in when it said out?'

'We just did,' said Naomi.

The car park was empty.

'We could have parked in here,' said Roger.

'It doesn't matter,' said Jade.

'No,' said Roger.

The gatehouse was a hexagon. It had tiny rooms. It was empty. They peered through the windows. Someone was decorating it.

'That's smaller than our house,' said Naomi.

'Is it a cottage?' said the boy.

'Yes,' said Naomi. He was swinging on her hand.

'Do we live in a cottage?' said the boy.

'Yes,' said Naomi.

'Why do we?' said the boy.

They were painting the panels of the hexagonal room

white. There was a cold cup of tea on top of a step-ladder.
'Picnic,' said Jade.

The wind hit them as they walked across the car park and left them as they stepped onto a narrow path through a small wood. There were bluebells and damp earth breathed at them. It was very, very quiet.

'It is spring,' thought Naomi, 'that's good. I am Sarah Bet and I wear beads, bells and bare feet to go to a party and then decide I won't. I sit cross legged on the floor. I switch on my electric fire that I painted, for fun, in the winter time. I fold my hands in my lap and wait to see who will come tip-tapping at the glass on my spring basement window. And if there is no one I will read a book and go to bed alone to dream of angels who will take me in their arms and do as I want them, and speak only when spoken to. My plants are stretching out of their pots and the white lawn of my spring sheets calls to me lovingly from the bed in the chimney-breast corner. I think of reading wanton songs and refuse. Watch the sickle through the window, read a page of the red book and succumbing to the bed's suggestion retire to cuddle myself inside my own arms.'

'Is this a jungle?' said the boy.
  'No,' said Naomi.
  'Are there lions?' said the boy.
  'No,' said Naomi.
  'Why?' said the boy.
  'We should find somewhere on the side of a hill and we'll be out of the wind,' Naomi called to Roger and Jade. They were ahead and John was with them.
  'Lions live in the jungle where it's hot,' said Naomi.
  'It's hot here,' said the boy.
  They were out of the wood. An arch covered in laburnum, not quite out. They twisted round a rose garden in bud. Roger was sweating profusely. He put his hand up to

his hair. It was wet. Six hairs came away on his sweaty palm.

The big house was newly painted and looked like a wedding cake kept too long in the shop. It confronted them.

'That's a funny house,' said the boy.

'It's big,' said Naomi.

'That's my house,' said Roger.

'It isn't,' said the boy.

'It is today,' said Roger. 'Come onto my lawn.' He pointed to a Henry Moore recumbent in dark wood.

'That's the gardener,' he said.

'It's a woman,' said the boy. 'I can see its titties.' An old lady sitting on a bench turned her head and looked at them. She had rings on every finger and a scarf on her head.

'Men don't have titties,' said the boy.

'Women can be gardeners,' said Naomi.

'This one wakes up on every second Tuesday and weeds the garden,' said Roger.

'It's a very big garden,' said the boy.

'She's a very big woman,' said Roger.

The boy looked at Roger and he looked at the figure. Roger was smiling.

'Yes,' said the boy. 'She is.'

Roger went on ahead. He was pleased. He skipped a little skip and the boy ran up to join him.

'Over there,' said Naomi pointing to a dip in the hill not far from a huge lake.

'Roger,' shouted Jade. He looked round. 'Over there,' she shouted.

Roger and the child veered sideways and up. They were enjoying themselves.

'Roger's got a spring in his step,' said Jade. John took her arm by the elbow as a gentleman would. John had long flowing hair in the early seventies. He'd had a beard and wore loon pants. Maroon. He'd lent Naomi his loon pants one day to go home when it was cold. In those days he'd liked her to wear his clothes. Now he was protective of his belongings and his hair was short. He wore combat trousers and square-cut bulky shirts and sometimes Naomi was afraid of him although even with her he was quiet and a gentleman.

'Look at me,' she thought. 'Oh please look at me.'

She brought up the rear. The child and Roger were already sitting in a perfect hollow. She looked down into the lake and she didn't like it much. It was black and looked as if the weed might suck you down. Rich house. Rich grounds.

'Look at me,' she thought. 'I need you.'

Jade spread out the rugs and the white linen table-cloth. It shone in the sun. She placed the Fortnum's picnic hamper at an angle to the corner of the table-cloth and before she opened the basket sat back on her heels and looked at her setting.

'Look, all of you,' she said.

John knelt down beside her. Roger stood behind. Naomi stood on her own.

'It's sparkling,' she said and supposed Jade had washed it by hand. 'We ought to give thanks,' she said, watching John worshipful and Jade caringly, gently, setting out the food with perfect hands.

'Who to?' said Roger looking up into the empty sky.

'Jade, of course. Thank you, Jade,' said John, taking a bunch of black, perfectly round grapes from Jade's perfectly white hands.

The boy ducked his head under Naomi's wide blue skirt and clung to her thighs.

'I like you,' he said, muffled under there. She put her hand on the cloth-covered head.

'I like you too,' she said.

'Daddy's silly,' said the voice.

Naomi looked at John. His eyes were still. He sat gracefully back on one heel, second leg bent, like a yoga god, back straight, head perfectly balanced, still grey eyes watching Jade, watching and watching.

'He isn't silly,' said Naomi.

'He is sometimes,' said the boy.

'He isn't now,' said Naomi. 'Come out from under there.'

The boy came out immediately. His hair was tousled and his cheeks were red.

'I like you best,' he said. 'Do you like me best?'

Naomi stroked her son's hair and put her arm round his shoulders lightly. 'I like you both.'

'I belong to you,' said the boy.

'You belong to no one,' she said, pulling him closer, head against her thigh. 'Do you want me to own you?'

'Yes,' the child replied, very firmly. He darted onto the rug and stole a black grape, then another.

'Those are for later,' said Jade. 'Open the wine, someone.'

Roger passed a corkscrew to John.

'Let him prove his virility,' he said. 'I run from mayonnaise jars, malt vinegar bottles, stuck tops of any description. It's enough to be a man. I don't feel any need to prove it.' Roger sat down. He watched John deal efficiently with the cork. He watched Jade pour wine into the red plastic beakers. He accepted wine from her. The red and white picnic stunned passers-by. The first mouthful of wine oozed out of Roger's pores. The sun shone on his grey velour track-suit top. It steamed slightly in the heat. He was embarrassed by his lack of wit. The child crawled over beside him and he slid the child a grape, the biggest, the roundest, the blackest he could find.

'*Déjeuner sur l'herbe*,' Naomi said and sat down. Her skirts floated out around her. She accepted wine from John.

'Thank you,' she said.

The sun shone on her. She looked her best in the sun. Her texture suited it. Jade looked at her.

'An advert for herbal shampoo,' she said. 'All that hair.'

'It's going grey,' Naomi said.

'Dye it.'

'No.'

'The skirt is delicious,' Jade said.

Their little group was attracting attention from all around. The dogs had smelt the beef. A man set up a swing ball next to them. Dark and in trainers, he played slowly in the heat. His baby watched from his pushchair and the au pair lay down on the grass.

'He's got a nice body,' said Naomi. She glanced at John. He was staring at the beef on the table-cloth and the great bowl of prawns and the kabanos. John and Naomi were vegetarians. He took a piece of beef. He took another. He piled his plate high with prawns.

'Everything's got to be eaten,' said Jade. Her plate was empty. She smiled at the others, the matriarch, keeper of secrets, mother of mysteries. Naomi took beef and prawns. John took a kabanos. Roger sloughed his way through a mound of everything and quaffed the clear wine. The boy ate only bread and grapes and drank only mineral water.

'What's over there?' he said.

'We're eating,' said John.

'Can we go over there?'

'Later,' said John.

'Have a kabanos,' said Jade.

'No,' said the boy.

'Thank you,' said Naomi.

'Thank you,' said the boy.

'Don't be silly, darling, it's only a sausage,' said Jade. The boy smiled at her. She smiled back at him.

'No, thank you,' he said.

'Jade, this is wonderful,' said John. 'You're a clever and beautiful woman.'

'Am I a woman?' she said and forked another piece of beef onto his plate. The centre was red. Roger ate lying on his side, Roman fashion, with steady skill.

'What makes a woman?' said Jade. 'When did we stop being girls?' She looked at Naomi, grey haired, sitting amongst her skirts, textured face, curls, brown eyes.

'Naomi's a girl. She always will be,' Jade said.

'How does the food get to your tummy?' the child asked Roger. 'It can't go down if you're lying like that.'

Roger sat up quickly and the wine instantly rose to his head. His belly shook sideways and he felt sick. He engulfed a quick couple of grapes.

'Those are for later,' Jade said.

His fingers burned as if a teacher had brought a ruler hard down across them. He looked at his wife. The child was watching him. Roger took another grape. Quite openly, with a smile on his face and sweat on his palms. He dug his fork back into the mound of food on his plate.

'You eat a lot,' said the boy admiringly.

'I like plastic,' Jade said. 'I have a dread that every house I walk into will be either Habitat or Laura Ashley. Where did you buy that skirt?'

'I made it,' Naomi said.

'What was the pattern?'

'I made it up.'

'I didn't know you had a machine.'

'I haven't,' said Naomi.

'You did that by hand?'

'Yes,' said Naomi.

'There must be six yards in that skirt.'

'Yes,' said Naomi.

'She's very clever,' said John.

'Have you enough bread?' Jade said to the child.

'Yes, thank you,' said the child.

'Would you like anything else?'

'Grapes please,' said the child.

Roger gave him the whole bunch.

'We have cake,' said Jade. 'Passion cake. Do you like cake?'

'No thank you,' said the child.

'Would you like to give the rest of the bread to the ducks?'

'Yes please,' said the child.

'When you've finished your grapes,' Jade said and she looked at Roger but the silk worm in his brain had gone back to sleep and his eyes had retired behind the pouches in his baby bland face. Jade said gently, 'Roger wake up,' but he didn't hear her. He stretched out on his side and asked the sun to dry his wet clothes.

'Coffee now or later? Cake now or later?' said Jade.

'A rest,' said Naomi.

John stood up. He held his hand out to his son. He gathered up the bread.

'Carry me,' said the boy.

John swept the child into his arms.

'Ducks,' he said. 'Jade, that was a wonderful picnic.'

'There's more to come,' she said, looking up at him in the sunlight. She watched him carry the child off. The sun shone on both their heads and they went down to the water.

The black mongrel belonging to the man with the swing ball and the au pair dropped a ball into Naomi's lap.

'Don't let him bother you,' shouted the man.

Naomi smiled. She pulled the dog's ears. They were warm silk in the palm of her hand.

'No bother,' she shouted back. The man had long straight legs, and a long straight back and a gypsy smile. Naomi put her hand under the dog's chin. She held its head up and looked into its brown eyes.

'Sit,' she said, very softly. The dog sat. Naomi picked the ball up and threw it far, far away.

'Good throw,' called the man.

Naomi smiled her own gypsy smile. The man's toddler son plonked down onto her lap and smiled up at her. He wound his hands into her hair.

'Hello,' she said.

'Don't be afraid to chuck him off if you get bored,' shouted the man.

'He's adorable,' she called back.

'Yes he is,' called the man.

The child let her hair go and sat quite happily in her lap.

'His name's Thomas,' called the man.

'Hello, Thomas,' said Naomi.

The dog flopped down beside her, panting.

'For heaven's sake,' said Jade.

'I don't mind,' said Naomi.

'That doesn't make it any better.'

Jade was wearing a long black shirt over her thermal vest. She was hot. She slipped her arms easily out of her shirt and slipped easily out of her thermal vest.

A jogger went past. He was completely bald with just tufts of hair sticking up. Diseased. He had bandages tight round his knees.

'If you have to do that to run, you shouldn't bother,' said Jade, back in her shirt. 'He looks most unhealthy.'

Roger woke. 'Where, where?' he said. 'I want to run,' he said. He stared at Naomi.

'Who's that?' he said pointing at the baby on her knee.

'Thomas,' said Naomi.

Roger glared at her suspiciously.

'Naomi's our little pied piper,' Jade said.

Over by the still black water John and the child dangled their feet over the edge and talked to the ducks. The ducks liked to be talked to and clustered round. John and the child threw their bread upon the water but the ducks weren't interested. Not a single duck ate a single crumb of bread. They tried to nibble the boy's toes. He laughed.

'Carnivores,' said John.

'What does mean carnivores?' said the boy.

'Meat eaters,' said John.

'Why did you eat the beef and the sausages?' said the boy. He had found some pebbles and was throwing them into the black lake. The ripples moved out and the ducks scattered.

'Rainbows,' said the boy.

'Why did you not?' said John.

'I'm not a vegetarian,' said the boy.

'It would have been rude for us not to eat the food,' said John. The boy looked at him. 'I wanted to,' said John. 'Is Jade pretty?'

The boy looked at him again.

'Yes,' he said.

'Do you like her hair?'

'Yes,' said the boy. 'Would she let me swing on it?'

'No,' said John.

'Naomi lets me swing on hers.' He glared at his father. 'Naomi's pretty.' He found a big stone and flung it out with all his might, far into the pond.

'I want to roll down the hill,' said the boy.

John swung the boy all the way up onto his shoulders.

'I used to carry you like this when you were little.' The boy was laughing and catching at the branches of trees.

'When I was a baby.'

'Not quite,' said John.

'When I was a toddler,' said the boy.

'That's right,' said John.

'Where do babies come from?'

It was a favourite question. The boy was always one for secret places and naked cuddles. He had little stroking hands that fluttered over arms and thighs.

'You were conceived in a purple room,' said John.

'Why?'

'It was my room. I liked purple. It had a fireplace and that was purple too. And a lampshade. I painted that purple. The sheets were purple and the blankets and the quilt.'

'Did Naomi like purple too?'

'I think so,' said John.

'I like purple,' said the boy.

They were at the top of the hill. John took the boy from his shoulders.

'You can take me to bed tonight,' the boy said.

'We'll be late,' said John.

'After my bedtime?' said the boy.

'Yes,' said John.

'After Laurie's bedtime?' Laurie was his best friend.

'Yes,' said John.

'Are you going to roll down the hill?' said the boy.

'No,' said John.

'Call Naomi,' said the boy.

John looked down from the hilltop. Roger was stretched out on the rug. The picnic was gone. Coffee and cake lay on the white tablecloth. He saw the child in Naomi's lap and the dog. He saw the dark man with the gypsy smile lay down his swing-ball bat. The au pair was asleep. Thin child-woman stretched out in a T-shirt dress, straight black hair fanned out in a peacock tail round her head, dark skin, red lips. The gypsy man left her and sat by Naomi. John watched him take Naomi's hand in his and kiss the inside of her wrist. Naomi laughed. He saw Jade twist her beautiful hair round her hand and pin it up, saw her stretch out her hand and the man merely shake it. He watched Jade bend her neck this way and that and flutter her white hands as she spoke. The opal gleamed out white sunfire and the gold shone dull and hopeful on her wrist and at her throat.

The man watched Naomi and flashed his gypsy smile at her.

'I'll roll down the hill with you,' John said.

'Why?' said the boy.

'For fun.'

'Come on then,' said the boy. 'You lie at my feet and I'll lie at your head.'

John rolled slowly. First he felt every stick and stone. Then he rolled faster. He rolled and rolled. He started to laugh. Beyond him the boy was laughing too. They crashed in a painless bundle at the bottom. The man lay on his back and threw the child into the air. Roger woke up. He saw them and winced with pain as he tried to move his left arm out from under him. He didn't take his eyes away from the child. Naomi stroked the little one's head in her lap. John clasped the child to him and rolled twice more with his son in his arms. Then he picked him up and carried him to the rug.

'Coffee,' he said. And Jade smiled at him slowly and looked to see if his eyes were still. Roger belched and cut slices of cake.

'Will you join us for coffee?' Jade asked the gypsy man. His white shoes were of softest leather and had 'hunger' painted in gold on the side.

'Thank you,' he said. 'Yvonne is asleep as you can see.' His accent was softly foreign, not French, not Italian. 'We are all being stared at. Have you noticed? Everyone coming past here is wearing thick sweaters and jackets. Beyond this hill there is a high wind. Down in this hollow we have summer.' He looked at the boy. 'Would you like to play with my swing ball?' The boy shook his head, unsure. 'Perhaps later you will play with your mother or your father.'

Roger handed the gypsy man a piece of cake. Roger objected to his brownness, objected to his leanness and didn't know why he paid so much attention to Naomi and none to Jade. Roger was sick of the sun.

'I'll play swing ball with you,' he said to the boy. 'With your permission of course.' He smiled at the gypsy man.

'It is quite energetic I think you will find.' The gypsy man smiled back at him.

'I'm not altogether unfit,' Roger said and pulled his velour top down as far as it would go. He wanted to cover the overhang of his bum so that it would not shake as he turned his back to the gypsy man and walked over to the swing ball.

'Come on,' he yelled to the child. The boy looked at Naomi.

'Go on if you want to,' she said.

'He's walking funny, Roger,' said the child.

'What?' Roger yelled.

'Nothing,' said Naomi.

'What did he say?' yelled Roger.

'He said you're walking funny,' yelled the gypsy man, smiling.

Roger skittled over to the bats. His heart was beating. He'd never been able to play tennis or badminton. The thought of squash made him sick. He wanted the child. He would be safe with the child. He looked back. They were all watching him. Their eyes were huge. Great bony faces leered at him. He picked up the bat, stood up. He was dizzy. The sun beat into his skull. Supposing he couldn't hit the ball. Supposing the ball hit him. Down the line of Roger's crutch sweat oozed. His pubic hair prickled the tops of his thighs. Supposing he hit the ball and jumping around made urine run out the top of his penis. Sudden exertion. Sometimes it happened. He'd be safe with the boy. Why didn't he come? Roger wanted someone to play with. He walked up to the swing ball, bent down, propped the bat against the stand. He straightened, let the dizziness take him. Looked across at the group, straight into the teeth of the gypsy man's smile.

'Going for a slash,' he yelled.

They waved. The sign was on the brow of the hill.

'Back soon,' he yelled, betrayed by the child.

They waved again. The backs of Roger's calves screamed at the first five yards of the hill. He wobbled. The slap of his thighs steadied him and he bent his weight into the effort of climbing. His foot slipped from under him and he landed heavily on one knee. It hurt. He dragged himself up, rubbed it a bit.

'You're not very good at it are you?' The child was beside him.

'What?' said Roger.

'Walking,' said the child.

'Coming with me?' said Roger.

'Yes,' said the child.

Roger smiled.

'They're talking down there,' said the child.

They looked back. The gypsy man was looking at his watch. They walked on up the hill and Roger put his hand on the boy's shoulder.

The gypsy man was looking at his watch.

'You were always so fiery,' said Jade. 'I remember you standing on the stage in hall, making speeches. I remember you leaning forward over the lectern and pointing a finger at us.'

'May I have another piece of cake?' said John.

'Of course.' Jade picked up the knife and forced it through the cake. Her knuckles shone white and the gold ran down her arm.

'I won a prize for that,' said Naomi.

'Take it easy,' said John and put his hand over Jade's on the knife.

'You must be very clever,' said the gypsy man.

'I was speaking for capital punishment. We were grammar school girls. Fee payers. Our parents were Conservatives to a man. Women didn't count. I've always been ashamed of it.'

'But you carried your point of view,' said the gypsy man.

'Their point of view,' Naomi said. 'I gave it back to them from a platform. Pat. Everything they'd taught me. So they gave themselves a prize.'

'I see,' said the man.

'I won one for dancing,' said Naomi. 'I was proud of that.'

'You have changed your view on capital punishment?'

The man was making conversation. Naomi watched the colour come into his dark skin. She watched his eyes as he allowed the lashes to make shadows on his cheekbones. The lashes were impossibly thick and tipped with gold. He swept them up and looked straight at her.

'Yes,' she said. 'Of course I have.'

The thin woman child, the au pair, rolled over onto her face. Her little bottom stretched above the grass.

'Her youth has tired her out,' the man said.

'What?'

'I am a romantic,' the man said.

'You're trying too hard.' Naomi bowed her head to the babe in her lap. The man laughed.

'Come with me for a walk,' he said. 'We will take the baby and the dog and you will be quite safe. Your husband will not mind. He will be caring for two beautiful people. A sleeping woman and a sleeping girl.'

'I'm wide awake,' said Jade.

'Come for a walk,' said the gypsy man. Naomi set the baby on his feet.

'Do you mind?' she asked John.

'Of course you are all welcome. I know these grounds well,' said the gypsy man.

'No thank you,' said Jade. 'I'm lazy today.'

'Then,' said the gypsy man, 'you have a duty to stay.'

John looked up at him, grey eyes still.

'I will take care of your wife,' said the gypsy man.

The boy was tired when he reached the toilet. He was panting. Roger's hand had been heavy on his shoulder. The toilet was set back at the top of the hill and covered in wistaria.

'A gazebo,' Roger breathed out. 'Bricked in. Made convenient.'

Roger's climb up the hill had induced his penis to let out water. He had a wet patch on the front of his track-suit trousers. Involuntary incontinence. Roger thought he could smell it.

'Coming in?' he said to the boy.

They stood in front of gleaming white urinals, seldom used but kept clean and smelling sweet with lemon verbena potted plants exuding their odour of calm disinfectant. The boy imitated Roger, sliding his penis out of his knickers because what he held was secret. They stood side by side and Roger's wee wouldn't come because the boy was staring and staring at his penis.

'That's very big,' said the boy.

Roger stood straighter.

'It's even fat,' said the boy.

A fat penis was something to be proud of.

'It's much bigger than John's,' said the boy.

Roger smiled a big smile and the pee came gushing out. The boy watched the great jet of water and added his trickle to the fountain.

'We could put out fires,' said Roger. 'I'll buy you an ice-cream. We'll take ice-cream back for everyone.'

'Can I have a double ninety-nine with strawberry sauce and chocolate sauce?'

'We'll have one each,' said Roger. 'Ice pole for Jade, raspberry ice lolly with ice-cream in the middle for Naomi. What does John like?'

'Choc ice,' said the boy.

Roger put his heavy hand round the boy's shoulder and felt him shrug at the weight of it. Roger's smile drooped and his hand grew stiff. He couldn't take it away. The boy gazed up at him.

'How do you get it in your trousers?' he asked.

Roger's hand relaxed and the boy's body accepted it.

'One-eyed trouser snake,' Roger dared to say and the boy gave a five-year-old's knowing laugh. They were friends.

'Why did the chicken cross the road?' said the boy.

'I don't know, why did the chicken cross the road?'

'Because it wanted to go on holiday,' said the boy.

Roger laughed and couldn't stop. The boy was pleased. They walked out of the toilet and up the pathway past three litterbins and followed a sign which said refreshments in Gothic script.

'*Déjeuner sur l'herbe*,' said the gypsy man. 'That was my favourite. I drew it in charcoal grey water-colour and pink. The grouping was exactly right. The woman disrobed. In the foliage around them were faces, tiny lettered poems. Very small. For the quick eye. Faint blue I used. Wine. A hand holding wine. A book. I set this back and over it I constructed a door of pure forest in my charcoal grey and pink. White. The background was white. The whole was made of wood. Into the door I put a lock. I used a recording device. Circular. Open the door and a scene is played out in conversation. In French. Triggered off by the lock mechanism. You actually listen to it. You understand. The woman says she is hot. She will take off her dress. It is stuck. Will the man help her? The man would like a joint. Shall they roll a joint? Is the stuff they have good? Is the wine good? A lazy conversation and behind it the songs of the birds of the wood. Close the door and it stops.'

'It sounds lovely.' Naomi bent. The lace of her underskirt was once more caught on the hook of her boot. The child was asleep in the pushchair. Rhododendrons blocked them off from all the other visitors to the big house. The gypsy man stooped to help her.

'Of course it is only a toy. But it was not there before I made it.'

'You're very clever.'

'Out of my toys for grown-up people, I make some money.'

'I'm sure.'

'There is no reason why grown-up people should not play.'

An old woman came round the rhododendron bushes. She was trailing behind her a shopping basket on wheels, tied with a blue bow and full of West Highland terrier.

'I'm glad you're both here,' she said. She had a gauzey blue scarf round her neck and the dog had a blue ribbon round its neck.

'I didn't want to meet a man on his own,' she said. 'You never know what they might do. I'm lost,' she said.

The gypsy man smiled at her very gently and veiled his dark eyes.

'From what are you lost?' he asked.

'I was expecting something else,' she said. 'Finsbury Park,' she said, 'where is it?'

'Many miles away,' said the gypsy man.

'How many?' the old lady asked, quite brightly.

'Twelve,' said the gypsy man.

'This'll do then,' said the old lady and trailed her basket on her way. Naomi was still kneeling, the gypsy man still beside her. He laid his eyelashes along his cheekbone.

'Grey-haired Madonna,' he said.

'It's not entirely grey.'

'It is beautiful. You are beautiful.'

'I'm stuck. If I stand up I'll rip my underskirt.'

He reached his hand to the top of her boot. He unhooked the lace and kissed it. He trailed his fingers up her leg and touched the wetness between her thighs.

'You and I should make a child,' he said.

Naomi began to cry.

There was a queue for ice-creams. Everyone was wearing German film directors' riding boots and heavy jumpers. They were sweating in the sunshine. The owners of the café had put tables out and were serving cream teas on a lawn strewn with last autumn's leaf fall. The owners of the café had dragged horse-drawn carriages onto the patio to interest the German visitors. They were covered in large notices telling children to keep off. The child looked once at the carriages and looked away.

'Once there were no cars,' said Roger standing in the queue.

'I know that,' said the boy.

'Wouldn't you like to ride in one?' said Roger.

'Have they got horses?' the boy asked.

'No,' said Roger.

There was silence between them. Roger removed his hand from the boy's shoulder and watched the German girls moving inside their suntans. In Roger's experience, all German girls were golden brown. The boy was watching a cat on the wall. The cat was grey and yowled at each person who passed. The boy went over to it and yowled back. The cat looked at him, quite silent, and stretched its head up to be stroked. The boy walked back to Roger, the cat followed.

'In our road we've got a cat like this,' said the boy. 'You can stroke it if you like.'

Roger was allergic to cats and sneezed at the thought of them. He sneezed now.

'Bless you,' said the boy and he tickled the cat's ear. Roger's eyes began to water. A tear ran down his cheek. At the ice-cream counter they had run out of change. The Germans were passing out twenty pound notes and the Greeks who owned the refreshments were cross in the heat. There was a musty smell from the horse-drawn carriages. Cat's piss. Roger could see the fleas hopping to and fro on the cat's back. The boy moved from foot to foot. Roger looked at the pictures on the front of the ice-cream counter. Ice pole, two double ninety-nines with chocolate and strawberry sauce, strawberry ice lolly with ice-cream in the middle and a choc ice, they did not exist. There was a picture of a drooling Dracula in dark sticky red for seventeen pence. Roger wore a little purse crosswise on his chest. It hung down on his left hip. He had a pound note and two pence, enough for six Draculas. Roger pushed his way to the front of the queue. The boy followed.

'Six Draculas,' said Roger, 'I have the right money.' He smiled at all the Germans. The Greek behind the counter smiled at him. The boy smiled at him as the lollies were passed over. Roger took one lolly and examined it carefully. He blew into the wrapper and the paper cover shot off. Roger turned it round carefully. The boy's face was very serious. Roger held the lolly out to him.

'This is good for you,' he said.

The boy took the lolly. Roger had a free hand. The boy had a free hand. The boy took Roger's hand. In his other hand Roger held five Dracula ice lollies melting slightly but he walked proud with his little purse banging empty on his left hip.

'I bought one for the man with the swing ball,' he said.

* * *

The gypsy man led Naomi, the child in the pushchair and the black mongrel dog into the empty heart of a cluster of rhododendrons. He managed it gracefully, without waking the child. The dog flopped down. The gypsy man took off his sweatshirt and his jeans. He wore no pants. Naomi watched him. The tears had stopped. The man in front of her was beautiful and she enjoyed watching him. He stood before her.

'Leave your clothes on,' the gypsy said. 'You are beautiful.' He moved across to her. He pushed up the front of her skirt. The lace of the underskirt fell away from her thighs. He touched gently the pubic hair inside her pants. He pushed the crutch of her pants aside and held it away from her vagina, stroking gently.

'We will make a baby.' Stroking, stroking. 'Do you want that?'

'Yes,' she said.

He put his penis softly up against the lips of her vagina.

'You are soft and warm,' he said and he picked at the opening of her own secret place with the tip of his penis. He lay her down. He pushed his penis full into her and lay still a moment.

'Will you come?' he said.

'Yes,' she said and he thrust hard into her, up against the bone and dark, deep inside her. There was nothing around her, nothing of her but him inside her. She clenched hard onto him, drew back from him and let him further and further in.

The red of the Dracula lollies was running down Roger's hand up to the sleeve of his track suit and he didn't care. The boy held tight to his other hand. The boy's face was covered in red dye. His lips, his mouth, the tip of his nose.

'How did you get ice lolly on the tip of your nose?' Roger said.

'Is it?' said the boy.

'Yes,' said Roger.

The boy stretched out his tongue to lick it off. 'Can't reach,' he said.

'I can,' said Roger and he stuck his tongue out of his mouth forever, curled the point up delicately and touched with absolute precision the very tip of his nose.

'Exie,' said the boy.

Roger put his tongue back in his mouth. 'Pardon,' he said.

'Excellent,' said the boy. 'I like you.'

'I like you too,' said Roger and he blushed and put his hand up to wipe his face and his hair. The hand with the lollipops, the bright red hand. He wiped Dracula juice down the left side of his face and stuck it on his hair. He took his hand away. There were five hairs stuck to the five lollipops. The boy was laughing. Roger couldn't quite decide whether it was funny or not.

'Are you cross?' said the boy.

'No,' said Roger but he was looking at the hair stuck to the ice lollies. The boy's hand slid out of his. The boy's face looked up at him but Roger couldn't smile.

John had his hand on Jade's ankle. It was slender and her leg was well shaved. Naomi's leg bristled with dark hair in the summer and cuts on the shinbone. In the winter she didn't shave them at all. John wanted a woman who was smooth, from her long thick hair to her darkly polished toes. Only the coffee remained of the picnic. The white table-cloth, the cake, the red plastic bowls, the picnic paraphernalia had been neatly packed in the hamper by Jade.

'Are you happy?' John said.

'Of course.'

'What's your name?' John said.

'Don't be silly.'

'Your real name,' John said.

'I don't remember.'

'Of course you do,' John said.

'Not if I don't want to.'

'Tell me,' John said.

'When we meet,' said Jade, 'when I think over the day

afterwards, I can remember what everybody has said, but not you. I have this picture of you sitting outside, very still, and judging all of us. Why have you got your hand on my ankle?'

John took his hand away.

'Why have you taken it away?'

'We could look over the house,' said John.

'Who would look after the picnic things?'

John pointed at the au pair, sleeping in the sun.

'Do you think he sleeps with her?' said Jade.

John looked at her.

'There, you see,' said Jade.

They gazed away from each other into the dark waters of the lake. On the opposite bank was a giant climbing frame, a scaffolding structure.

'They do the 1812 over there with fireworks,' said Jade. 'Your son might like that.'

John didn't answer.

'Don't sulk, John,' she said. 'It doesn't suit you.'

'Do you suppose she's all right?' said John. 'She's been asleep for a very long time.'

'Perhaps she's been making love all night.'

'She's very still,' said John.

'Wake her if you're worried.'

Again they were silent. John was studying the sleeping girl.

'Come on then, we'll go to the house,' Jade said.

'We had better not leave her.'

He watched the girl. Her skin was very pale. Her hair was black and shiny. Her skin had no line upon it. The T-shirt cotton of her dress moulded into the shape of her body.

'We'd better stay here,' he said.

Jade put her hand upon his arm. 'Look,' she said, 'isn't he a darling?' She pointed to a black alsatian. The dog plumed its legs out into a trot.

'He knows he's being watched, the pet.'

The dog's master threw a ball. The dog caught it in mid air.

'He's a clever one.'

A white West Highland terrier joined the alsatian. It wore a blue bow.

'Oh the sweetie. John he's a cheeky one. Watch him.' The West Highland terrier ran under the alsatian's legs. The alsatian dropped the ball, the West Highland terrier picked it up.

'There's a dobermann up there. Can you see. Two of them.' Jade was excited.

The two dobermanns rolled over and over and laid their two heads on an old man's lap.

'Ah, they're gentle. See John, they're gentle. Where's his ribbon, the little pet. Did he come out without his ribbon, then.'

She pointed to a Yorkshire terrier stepping high over blades of grass. 'The sweetheart. Shouldn't let him out without his ribbon.'

'I must wake her,' said John.

Jade reached out her hand. She touched John. She put her hand on his. She looked down at their joined hands.

'Let her be, John. You'll frighten her to death if you wake her. She probably doesn't even speak English.'

She looked down at their joined hands and left her hand in his and her eyes cast down.

'I'm sorry. Look there. Look there. He's a clever lad then.'

A labrador pup retrieved a stick and dropped it at his owner's feet. The dog lolloped round and round in ecstasies of joy and delight. Its too-big paws flopped onto the grass and its tail waved out wildly from side to side. Jade laughed.

'Of course,' she said, 'my name was Mary.'

'I don't sleep like that.'

'We're not all like you.' She said it without sharpness and she did not remove her hand.

'I've got presents for you to take home,' she said. 'You're to have the picnic hamper. I've bought some hair gel for Naomi. She can make little curls in her hair. Straighten it. Anything she likes. I've bought her a silver boob tube. She has such lovely shoulders. It was in Peter Jones' sale. Very cheap. Naomi suits silver. We never use the hamper. Then of course there's the Beast, the yoghurt beast, you know. I told Naomi. It's the culture, the real thing. Of course it might be dead. It's been frozen for months but they do say it'll last for up to a year frozen. Of course if it's dead I can always get some more.' Her fingers squeezed his tightly and the opal ring hurt his hand.

'A woman at work gave it to me. I do three days a week now. All my friends know, Mondays and Fridays I'm at home. They must phone me. I hate the phone. You know that, don't you? You know I hate the phone. The woman, my working companion, she's Chinese. It's a charity organization. I don't work for nothing. I don't mean that. I work for the charity. It became imperative for me to leave the house. There was talk at one time of my modelling, for *Vogue*, face not body. Of course I couldn't. I thought all I had to do was to be beautiful. I listen to Radio 4. The World Service and Radio 4. The best news is on the World Service. My Chinese working companion gave me the culture, the beast. She used to live in Switzerland. The beast came from Russia. Really. A dissident got out. Some such thing. He brought the beast with him. Didn't bring much but he brought that. It grows, you see. Feeds on the milk that makes the yoghurt so it grows unless you touch it with metal, then it dies. I don't want it, or if I change my mind she can give me some more.'

'Jade,' he said.

'I'm not kind, I'm not, I'm not. You mustn't say I'm kind. The yoghurt was too bitter for me and it's just the sort of thing Naomi would like. I know it is. It depresses me. John. Do you realize it's always been alive. I can't bear the thought of it.'

'Jade,' said John.

'The hamper. We'd have given that to a jumble sale. You should have it. Naomi would like it. You're the people who should have it.'

'Hush now,' said John. 'Hush now.'

From the top of the hill, the boy and Roger looked down at John and Jade holding hands on the rug.

'Would you like to roll down the hill?' said the boy.

'I've got these,' said Roger.

'You are cross,' said the boy.

They stood there side by side, a fat man holding five runny ice lollies and a boy with a sticky face. Roger wanted to cry. He was covered in stick and sweat and he could feel the snot of unshed tears building up in his throat and his nose. He sneezed.

'Bless you,' said the boy.

A gob of green snot depended from Roger's nose. He wiped it on his sleeve.

'Haven't you got a hankie?' said the boy.

'No,' said Roger.

'Neither have I,' said the boy and he wiped his own nose on his sleeve.

'No one'll want these,' said Roger.

'I do,' said the boy.

'So do I,' said Roger. He sat down at the top of the hill. He blew the paper off two ice lollies. He handed one to the boy and took one himself. He let the paper blow where it wanted, spoiling the landscape. He licked the lolly. He smeared his lips with its red stickiness. He dopped some on the end of his nose. The boy laughed.

'Will you roll down the hill with me when we've finished our lollies?' the boy asked.

A gentleman with a shooting-stick walked past. He speared the ice-lolly wrappers with the tip of his stick.

'It is imperative,' he addressed himself to Roger, 'that one brings up one's children to respect the rights of the people by whom one is surrounded. Imperative. There is no point in your denying these are yours, sir. I saw you let them go, sir. With my own eyes, sir. You and your son, sir. You are blots on the landscape. Blots on the landscape.'

The man walked off with the ice-lolly papers on the end of his shooting-stick. Roger put his thumb to his nose and waggled his fingers.

'Come on, Blot,' he said to the boy, 'bet I can finish my two before you finish your two.'

'There's one over,' said the boy.

'The one who finishes his two first gets it.' Roger wrapped

his tongue round a Dracula lolly.

'Will you roll down the hill with me?' asked the boy. 'After these.'

'We'll be sick,' said Roger.

'I won't,' said the boy.

'He'll be sick,' said Jade.

'Who?' said John. Jade was still holding his hand.

'Roger,' said Jade. 'He's up at the top of the hill eating ice lollies.' She flicked a fly from her arm, killing it with one long red nail.

'Damn,' said Jade. 'I didn't mean to kill it.'

'She'll burn,' said John. 'Will you wake her? She won't be frightened of you.'

'Roger's frightened of me. One morning he'll wake up and see a line at the corner of my mouth or a grey hair. He won't like it and he's afraid. I am too.'

She took cream from her bag and rubbed it into her hands. She glanced her hands lightly over her face. She took a white floppy hat from her bag. It had a wide brim. She put it on. Her face was in shadow out of the sun. She reached her hand out and touched John's arm. 'Take off your shirt,' she said. 'It's very warm.'

John unbuttoned his shirt, pulled it out of his trousers and took it off.

'Isn't that better?' she said. 'Do stop worrying about that silly girl.'

She put her hand on his bare arm. The opal gleamed out. His skin was golden, her hand was white.

Roger watching from the top of the hill finished his first ice lolly and quite methodically started on his second.

'It strikes me, young Blot,' he said, 'that the last ice lolly is mine anyway. You've already had one.'

The boy looked at him.

'If you finish first I'll roll down the hill,' said Roger. His eyes were on the rug below. The boy smiled.

* * *

'Naomi's been gone for a long time,' said John.

'Is she enjoying herself, do you think?'

'I've got to wake that girl.'

'Take my hand, John.'

He moved away from her and sat still on the farther side of the rug. He couldn't stop watching the girl. He wanted to see her chest rise and fall with each breath but she was too far away. He wanted to hear her breathe, but he couldn't.

'Stop worrying.'

'What do you want, Jade?'

'Can I have the moon? Will you give me that, please? You had your hand on my ankle.'

'It was a mistake.'

'I see.'

'I'm sorry I find you very attractive I always have but . . .'

'I see. You make advances to me, I respond, you slap me in the face.'

'Roger's watching from the hill.'

'Have you ever committed a criminal act?' said Jade.

'What?'

'You obviously think that man with the smile has done something to the girl.'

'She doesn't wake up.'

'And now he's doing something to your wife.'

'It sounds ridiculous,' said John.

'I hardly think a murderer would sit with us eating cake and drinking coffee with his son and his mongrel dog then go off for a walk leaving a dead girl on the grass. She's sleeping. What's wrong with you, John?'

'I stole some books once. No twice. Once from a station bookstand. Once from a bookshop. It terrified me.'

'I stole a bra. It was very brief and very lacy. I went into the shop with no bra on. I didn't intend to steal one. It was just coincidence. Sometimes I wear a bra, sometimes I don't. Today I'm not. Well, I had on thermal underwear. I tried this bra on, decided I might as well not take it off. It was a delicious little thing, two slight triangles of lace. I have good muscles. I don't need too much support. I walked up to the counter intending to pay and the girl looked at me absolutely blankly. I smiled at her and walked out of the shop. I felt euphoric. Please let us be friends.'

'Go and wake that girl.'

There was a screaming at the top of the hill, shrill and high. Roger and the boy ran down with arms outstretched. They were aeroplanes. The boy thumped down onto the rug.

'I won, I won.'

Roger careered to and fro droning and panting.

'He won. He won.'

He divebombed the boy on the rug.

'Whizz me round,' shouted the boy. 'Whizz me round, Daddy.'

John picked the boy up by his ankles and hurled him round in a fast circle off the rug onto the grass up into the air and down.

'Again, again.' The boy was laughing and panting. John tickled him.

'Hold your arm up. I told you to hold your arm up,' John was stern. The boy held up his arm. 'So that I can tickle it,' said John.

'Uncle, Uncle,' shouted the boy.

His father took him into his arms and babied him round in a fast circle. He dropped him gently down onto the rug.

'Again, again,' shouted the boy.

'That's quite enough,' Jade said. John sat down on the mat.

'Again John, please.'

John lifted the boy's T-shirt and blew on his belly. The boy giggled and giggled.

Roger picked him up by the ankles. He hadn't meant to but the boy was hanging upside down and Roger's arms were aching with the strain of holding him there. He couldn't think what to do next.

'Put me down,' the boy gasped.

'For goodness sake take him off the rug,' Jade said. Roger began to turn.

'Off the rug, Roger, you're too close to us,' Jade was shouting.

Roger could feel John hovering.

'Put me down.' The boy sounded frightened, though there was still a laugh in his voice.

Roger turned faster. His arms were aching, burning. His hands were loosening round the boy's ankles.

'Move away,' Jade cried.

Roger tried to tighten his grasp. His hands wouldn't work. The boy crumpled to the ground. He bumped his head on the picnic hamper. John gathered him into his arms.

'How could you be so stupid?' Jade said.

The boy was sobbing.

'Oh my God. Oh my God,' said Roger. He flopped onto his knees beside the boy and his father.

'Oh my God.' He pawed at the boy with a loose floppy hand. The boy hid his face in his father's chest. Roger was panting for breath and the boy sobbed on.

'I'm sorry. I'm sorry. I'm sorry,' Roger panted. 'Look,' he said, 'I'll make it up to you. I'm sorry. We'll roll down the hill. We'll roll down the hill together. I promise. I promise.'

The boy sobbed on but he turned his head and Roger saw the great graze in the middle of the boy's forehead. Roger put out his hand. Very, very gently he touched the place beside the hurt.

'Oh,' he said, 'I'm sorry.'

A tear ran through the sweat and the sticky ice-lolly mess on Roger's face. Jade reached inside her bag. Wrapped in a piece of clear plastic she had a wet face-cloth. She washed Roger's face with it. Some of the stick came off, not all of it. He was still crying.

'You'll have to wash your face in the lake,' she said.

John cradled his son in his arms. The girl in the T-shirt dress had not awakened. The boy sobbed on.

Naomi lay with her skirts above her waist in the rhododendron grove. The baby in the pushchair was still asleep. Something had disturbed the black mongrel. It lay with its head on its paws softly growling. The gypsy man was fully dressed. He sat beside Naomi smiling his gypsy smile. He held her hand.

'Blot,' Roger said to the boy, 'Blot I'll roll down the hill with you. Don't cry, Blot. We'll roll down the hill together. Don't cry, Blot. Don't cry.'

Roger tried to pull the boy into his arms but John held him tight and the boy held on to John.

The gypsy man smiled. Naomi's dress covered her. The gypsy man held her hand.

'Long ago,' he said, 'I was in the south of France with a very good friend of mine. Both of us. It was the first time we had been away from home. My friend and I. He was from your country. His name was Tom. We had been pen pals. Those things that schools arrange. You will write to him or you will write to him. However with us it was very successful. We spent holidays together. Exchange. You know. I with him. He with me. He was very dark, this Tom, like me. You would have thought we were twins. Naomi, are you listening to me?'

He squeezed her hand.

'I thought you were not listening to me. We left our separate schools. Our parents gave their blessing to us for a holiday completely on our own for as long as we liked until we once more had to enter the various educational institutions chosen for us. I, the Sorbonne, he Edinburgh. We lazed on beaches. We were very close. When we wanted to move, of course we hitched. We decided to go to Italy. We were some miles outside Nice when a limousine picked us up. In it was a very beautiful woman. Not young. "Where are you going?" she asked us. "You must come with me to my house," she said, "and you will be my guests for the night. I will feed you and tomorrow I will take you on your way." What should we have done? We went with her. Her house was above Nice, on a hillside surrounded by trees. It was very large. Totally black inside and out.

We walked from the hall into the dining-room. The table was already set, the guests already seated. It was the Last Supper, laid out exactly as Da Vinci painted it. In Christ's place was the figure of death. They were waxworks. We were asked to sit opposite them and our hostess bade us eat. The meal was superb. During it, she entertained us with tales of the lore of the district. The ancient lore, both dark and light. She read our faces. For Tom she predicted a good life and a happy one, comfortable, undisturbed. She said he was lucky. Me. She told me I was capable of great good or great evil. The bedrooms were black. Tom and I did not care to sleep in separate rooms. There had been an implication that she would visit us in the night. We were both afraid. Nobody knew where we were. We had gone off with a stranger. It is best not to trust strangers too much, Naomi. She came in the night. She sent Tom back to his own room. Very sweetly. Very kindly. So that he felt his fears had been ridiculous. Then she made love to me. In the morning the limousine took us across the border. It had orders to take us where we wanted to go. We left it as soon as, politely, we could. It was not the same for Tom and me after that. I had been picked out for a higher destiny. Of course it was just an ageing, still beautiful woman who desired one and not the other. We spoke once of that night. We said to each other how frighteneing it had been to eat with the figure of death at the table and then we never spoke of it again. Of course we had been lovers, Tom and I, but, Madonna, you will have guessed that.'

The baby awoke and yelled out its hunger. The gypsy man smiled. He dropped Naomi's hand.

'There my litte love.'

He took the baby out of the pushchair.

'We will find you some food.'

He chucked the baby once up into the air. It gurgled at him. He strapped it back into the pushchair. He took the dog lead in his hand. He pushed the chair to the edge of the hollow rhododendron grove.

'Naomi.'

The gypsy man smiled. He waved a hand and walked

on. Naomi had not moved. She lay quite where she was. Quiet.

'I can't stop crying,' the boy wailed. Jade tugged at John's sleeve. She tugged and tugged again.

'She should have woken up,' she said.

'Who?' said Roger.

'We've been making an awful lot of noise.'

John looked across at the au pair girl. She was paler than ever and the sun was blazing in a clear afternoon sky. They were protected in the lea of their hill.

'Go and waken that girl, Roger. She'll burn in the heat of this sun,' Jade said.

'No,' said John.

Jade glared at him.

'Roger,' he said, 'why don't you both go round the house?'

'Take the Blot round the house?'

The boy sobbed a huge end-of-crying-session sob.

'Come round the house with me, Blot,' said Roger.

The boy heaved a last sigh for luck. He let Roger pull him away from his father.

'When we come back,' the boy said, 'can we roll down the hill together?'

'We'll do it now, Blot.' Roger leapt to his feet.

'Take the boy round the house,' John said. 'Hills are more fun at the end of an expedition.'

Roger held out his hand.

'Blot,' he said. 'You coming?'

The boy stood up.

'Are you going to take care of me?' he said.

'There's hunting pictures in there,' Roger said, 'and buckles for eighteenth-century shoes.'

'What's eighteenth century?' the boy said and he took Roger's hand.

'They're silver and filigree,' said Roger. The boy nodded his head and they walked off together towards the icing-sugar house on the hilltop.

'Pretty girl that,' said Roger as he passed the au pair.

'Got to learn to know a pretty girl. Pale, though. Strange that in this sun.'

'Georgina's my girl friend. She's in my class at school. She's taller than me and she's got blue eyes. She cried at my party.'

John watched the two of them. He'd wanted to take the boy to the house himself.

'All right,' Jade said. 'You wake her.'

'Let them get further away,' John said, looking after the boy and Roger. They were still hand in hand. Then they stopped. Roger gave the boy a piggy-back.

'Naomi carries him like that,' John said, 'to school, to the shops. Sometimes he falls asleep on her back.'

'It can't be good for her.'

'Why not?'

'The boy's heavy, John.'

'She's strong.'

'Are you going to wake that girl?'

'Supposing we can't wake her.'

'Who would kill an au pair?'

'It could be drugs, of course,' John said.

'She could be asleep,' Jade said. 'But we don't think she is, do we?'

John got up from the rug. He walked over to the girl. He stood over her. She was beautiful, this au pair. Great lashes fanned her cheekbones. Her skin was translucent. There was a tiny scar at the corner of one eye. He couldn't see her breathing.

'Go on,' Jade called.

John looked at her. Smooth as when they entered the flat that morning but a waspish line at the corner of her mouth. Her hands fluttered and stabbed and were never still. The opal ring pointed out fire. John bent down on one knee beside the girl's head. He touched the edge of her straight black hair. It was cool in the sunlight. John felt hot all over. He bent. He kissed her cold lips.

Roger was puffing when he arrived at the icing-sugar house.

'Old buildings,' he said to the boy, 'they're better when they're dirty. This looks like a tart at a party.'

'Where's Naomi?' said the boy. 'She likes houses. The top class goes to Hampton Court on the boat.'

'Where do you go?' said Roger.

'We go to a farm,' said the boy. 'I went to a farm the first year I was at playschool and the second year I was at playschool and now I'm in Reception and I'm going to a farm.'

They walked past a long roofed patio with windows behind it. It was very hot. On the patio were two rows of chairs. Each chair was occupied by an old person of obviously foreign extraction with gold at their necks and in their teeth.

'Why are they sitting there?' asked the boy.

The old people were chattering. They lifted their hands, they bowed their heads, their bodies moved to and fro. The sound of their voices clattered up to the roof of the patio and bounded out into the rose garden. The boy slid down from Roger's back and chased a pigeon.

'Naomi says supposing a great big pigeon came down from the sky and chased you.' The boy smiled. 'There are no giant pigeons though,' he said. 'I know.'

'How?' said Roger.

'What?' said the boy.

'Because you've never seen something doesn't mean it doesn't exist.' Roger felt pleased with himself.

'Naomi says that,' said the boy. 'But there aren't any big pigeons. I know.'

'Falcons are big,' said Roger.

'And eagles,' said the boy.

'And ostriches,' said Roger.

They passed free through the entrance of the house.

'And horses,' said the boy.

'A horse can't fly,' said Roger.

'Pegasus,' said the boy.

The girl's mouth opened. It opened wider and wider. John leapt away. She was hideous. Her head lolled back loose on her neck. Her eyes rolled white. There was utter silence. The girl screamed. Long rolling screams. She screamed and screamed and the screaming brought John to his knees. People looked from all around.

'You silly bloody idiot,' Jade shouted. He was white. She ran over to him. The ring with the opal fire and the hand that wore it slapped across the girl's mouth. The screaming stopped. The people turned away.

'Go and get my bag,' Jade said.

John heard nothing.

'My darling John, go over to the rug and bring my bag over here.'

John got up. His legs shook and his feet flopped loose at the ankles. He walked over to the rug.

'I'm going to take my hand away,' Jade said. 'We thought you were dead. You've been asleep for hours. We thought you were in trouble. We wanted to help.'

The girl's eyes were dark and huge. Her face was grey.

'I have wet myself,' she said. 'I have shit my pants.'

John handed Jade her bag.

'I'm going to put some drops on your tongue. You've had a shock. This,' she said, unscrewing the top of a small bottle, 'is Rescue Remedy invented by a certain Dr Bach. It is essence of flowers in brandy. It will do you no harm.'

Jade held the dropper out to the girl. 'Open your mouth,' she said. She put the drops into the girl's mouth. John stood by. The clouds were rolling up, pushed by the hidden wind.

'I'm sorry,' he said to the girl.

'Go and bring me the rug and the table-cloth,' Jade said.

John did as he was told.

'You are beginning to smell,' Jade said. 'I will wrap you in the rug. No one will see what has happened. We will go to the toilet and fix you up. Are you French?'

The girl nodded. John brought the rug and the table-cloth. The girl was crying.

'Come along,' said Jade. 'No time for that. Open your mouth.'

She popped some more drops on to the girl's tongue.

'What's your name?'

'Yvonne.'

Jade wrapped the travelling rug around her and pulled her to her feet. Yvonne hung her head.

'Hold your head up,' Jade said.

They walked up the hill to the little house covered in wistaria. John sat down beside the picnic hamper. He stretched his hand out in front of him. It was shaking. His head was shaking. He lay down on the grass and closed his eyes. He wanted Naomi. He wanted her.

'If you walk straight with your head up,' said Jade, 'no one will even look at you. Why shouldn't you wear a travelling rug. That's the attitude.'

'I smell,' the girl said.

Jade put her arm round the girl's shoulders. 'We'll fix it. Patience. It's going to be all right.'

They walked, Jade's arm around her shoulders. Inside the ladies' loo there were two old women with jangling charm bracelets, slightly fat. They glanced at Jade and Yvonne. One of them threw her nose up into the air and sniffed. Jade held Yvonne closer. The old woman sniffed again and looked at her companion. Jade stared at the two thoroughly washing their hands at the basins. Rubbing the soap in, massaging it in. Gold rings beside the taps. Rubbing the soap in between their fingers, examining the fingernails, rubbing. The hands going round and round. Rinsing. Jade stood quite still pressuring the women to get out. Rinsing again. Hands held under the running water. Massaged. Round and round. Examined for any scrap of soap, passed inspection. The toilets had paper towels, roller towels, and air driers. The women opted for the paper towels. The bin was to one side of the basins. The women were afraid for their gold rings. Took a wide stance between the paper towels and the waste bin. Old yellow eyes darting. One towel to take the first moisture from the hands. Dab, Dab. Into the waste bin. A second towel between the fingers, round the wrists. A third towel pressed to the palms, round the back of the hands. Silent but breathing all the time. A fourth to make sure. Back to the basins, the rings by the taps and the handbags underneath. Hand cream. Each carried her own. Helena Rubenstein. Estée Lauder. From the right hand to the left, a drop in the palm, the bottle dextrously replaced in the bag, cupping the liquid preciously in the left hand. The left hand washing over the right. Jade stepped closer to the basins behind the women in the mirrors. The charm bracelets chinked as the hands wound round and round, rubbing in the unguents of forgotten youth. The women watched Jade in the mirror. Rubbed and rubbed. Examined the hands. Rubbed the last moisture into claw fingers and blue rope veins. Splayed the fingers, sighed, replaced the rings one by one. Examined the hands. Patted the hair, stiff with lacquer, pulled at dresses, real silk, Italian print, English tailored. And thus straightened out walked past Jade and out of the loo.

'What a strange pair,' Jade heard them say.

'So menacing.'

Jade shut the main door to the public conveniences. She put the waste bins up against it and the sanitary towel bins from the cubicles. She took the rug from the girl's shoulders. She turned on the water in each of the three basins. She put the plugs in the plug holes.

'Take off your dress.'

Silence.

'For God's sake don't be shy.'

The girl was crying.

'Go into the cubicle. Take some towels. Pass your dress out to me.'

She gave the girl towels and pushed her into a cubicle.

'For goodness sake, Yvonne. It washes off.'

'I'm ashamed.'

Jade kissed the girl's cheek.

'Hurry up. We're stinking the place out.'

The girl shut the door.

'Give me the dress. Quickly.'

The dress slid under the door. Jade put it into a basin. She scrubbed at it with the kindly provided bars of public convenience soap.

'What shall I do with my pants?'

'Flush them down the loo.'

The girl pulled the flush.

'I am a mess.'

'Have your knickers gone?'

'Yes.'

'There now. That's good fortune. They could have stuck. Clean yourself up with the towels.'

Jade soaked some towels and passed them under the door. She scrubbed at the dress, wrung it out, twisting at it strongly. She transferred the dress to the second sink and let the water out of the first. She scrubbed with the soap.

'Are you all right?'

'I am managing very well, thank you.'

'Keep pulling the flush. Don't let the loo block. When you're finished, come out here.'

Jade turned the taps in the first basin back on, left the dress soaking and cleaned out the basin with a paper towel. The girl pulled the flush.

'I have nothing on.'

'Come out here. I have a cloth, you can wash yourself properly.'

'I have nothing on.'

Jade squeezed the dress out and transferred it to the third basin. She swished it round with her hand and pulled the plug out from the second. She squeezed the dress out. Twisted it. Squeezed it. Washed the second sink round and put the dress for a last rinse into the first.

'Come out,' she called to Yvonne.

'If I still have shit on me . . .'

'I'll wash it off.'

She swished the dress round. She filled the second basin and let the water out from the third. She squeezed the dress out, thoroughly, so that there wasn't a drip.

'Blot,' said Roger, 'we've been up and down here six times.'

'Five,' said the boy.

They were standing at the top of a broad staircase.

'Look at this painting,' said Roger.

The boy was half-way down the stairs again.

'I like this house,' he said. 'Wish we had stairs like this in our house.'

'Stairs this size you'd have no house,' Roger said. They were on the way back up. He was clinging on to the banister.

'My friend Dafyd, he's got a big house,' said the boy.

Roger sat down on the top stair. The attendant at the door looked up at him. Roger stood up again.

'You smell,' the boy said.

'I'm hot,' Roger said.

'I'm sweaty,' the boy said.

Roger put both his hands on the boy's shoulders.

'Look at this picture,' Roger said. 'There are two boys in it.'

'Naomi takes me to see the tiger in the thunderstorm in the jungle up in London, then we feed the pigeons. It's a very frightened tiger.'

'Do you like that?' said Roger.

'I like feeding the pigeons. Naomi buys the pigeon food before we get on the train, from the shop that sells plants and smells funny and we have more than anyone else and the pigeons come to us because they know.'

'Do you chase them?' Roger asked.

'Naomi says they have to eat first,' said the boy.

'There are two boys in this picture,' said Roger.

'Oh yes,' said the boy and he passed on.

The picture was of two fat ponies ridden by two boys. There were dogs running with the ponies and the boys had guns over their shoulders and dead birds in one hand. Roger liked the picture. The sky was grey and lowering. He wanted the boys to get home before the storm.

The boy wasn't interested in the eighteenth-century buckles and neither was Roger. They found a necklace in the jewellery section the boy liked. It was silver filigree.

'Naomi's got one like that,' he said, 'but it shines more.'

'Where are the beds?' asked the boy. He wandered up a corridor and before Roger could stop him he knocked on a door marked private. There were plants in front of it but the chain which cut it off from the public area was down. A man opened the door.

'Good God,' said Roger.

'Good God,' said the man and neither of them was pleased.

'What are you doing here?' said Roger. The man had done Fine Art at University and been very big in student politics. Roger had been very dilatory. He couldn't remember the man's name.

'I can't ask you in,' the man said. 'I'm visiting.'

Roger looked at him. He calculated that he, of the two, had slightly the more hair. The man was fuzzy, pale and wore glasses. He was small.

'You're looking well,' said Roger.

'So are you.'

'Jade's down there near the lake,' said Roger.

'Give her my love,' said the man. The boy pulled at Roger's hand. He didn't like the house.

'This yours?' the man said, pointing at him.

'No,' said Roger.

'Thought not,' said the man. 'Couldn't see you two with kids.'

'Belongs to Naomi. You remember Naomi.'

The man smiled.

'Give her a big kiss from me. Say Peter sends his fondest love.'

Peter Stevenson. Roger placed him absolutely. Edited the student rag. Positively they had never got on. Naomi used to write articles about prophylactic vending machines in the women's loos. There weren't any. Naomi had been militant. Peter Stevenson bent down and kissed the boy.

'You give that to Naomi,' he said. 'You look like her.'

'Well,' said Roger, 'must get on.'

They faced each other for a couple of dry seconds.

'Keep in touch,' Roger said.

The man slid in behind the private door.

'Nice seeing you,' he said. The door shut. Roger charged off down the corridor. The boy had to run to keep up with him.

'No beds,' Roger said.

They passed a picture of a hunting group with a falcon.

It was in the dark corner of a staircase just before the exit. The boy stopped.

'That's a falcon,' he said.

'Come on,' Roger said and tugged at the boy's hand. There was a starling beneath the falcon's talons.

'Will it kill that little bird?' the boy asked.

'Probably,' Roger said. He pulled at the boy again.

'Why?' said the boy.

'Come on, Blot,' Roger said.

'The man's holding his arm out.' The boy was pointing into the picture.

'That's right,' Roger said. He was still tugging.

'Why?' the boy said.

Roger tugged him away from the picture.

'You're not being very nice,' the boy said.

Roger needed air. He tugged the boy past the old people chattering on the patio. He tugged him into the rose garden. He bumped down onto a bench.

'You'd think,' Roger said, 'he could have given us a cup of tea.'

The boy climbed up onto the bench beside him.

'Why did the man in the picture have his arm out like that?' he asked.

A bird hopped down beside Naomi in the rhododendron grove. It hopped right up to her hand. It looked at her and flew away. Naomi didn't move.

The red T-shirt dress hung on the louvre windows getting the breeze. Two of the sinks were empty and gleaming. The girl was standing in front of the mirror at the third while Jade worked on her body. The cloth was squeezed and soaped. Jade began under the girl's hair at the nape of her neck. She took the cloth out over the shoulders to left and right, down the girl's back. There was a mole in the middle. Jade panted a little, she washed vigorously. She brought the cloth down over the girl's buttocks and between, into the groove where the mess had been.

'You're quite, quite clean,' she said. 'We'll wash your whole body. You'll feel better for a good wash.'

She washed the girl's legs, between the thighs at the back. The girl was very still. Jade rinsed out the cloth and washed off the soap. She dried the girl's back and legs with paper towels. One to take off the moisture. Two to pat her dry.

'Would you like to do the front yourself?' Jade asked.

'You are making me feel better.' The girl was staring into the mirror.

'It's all over,' Jade said. 'You're all right.'

'Why did he kiss me?' the girl asked.

Jade soaped the cloth and washed the girl's arms and breasts.

'You are beautiful,' she said.

The girl was crying again. Jade washed her belly and the fronts of her legs.

'You'll make your eyes red,' she said. She rinsed the cloth and wiped off the soap.

'You haven't washed me there,' the girl said. She pointed to her genitals. 'I am dirty.'

Someone tried the handle of the door. Jade threw herself against it. 'We are out of order,' she said.

The girl laughed. The people outside rattled the handle. Jade could hear them tutting. They tip-tapped away on their high-heeled shoes. The girl was giggling. Jade soaped the cloth once more.

'There,' she said. The girl stopped laughing. Her eyes travelled over Jade's body. Jade smiled.

'There,' she said. She handed the girl the cloth. 'You can manage yourself now.'

She turned her back. She took the belt from around the waist of her long black shirt.

'You won't be able to wear your dress,' she said. 'We'll take it out in the sun. It'll dry quickly. You can wear this until it's dry.'

The girl's hand touched her bare shoulder. Jade turned round. The girl looked at her breasts and her hand slid down to Jade's waist.

'You have been very kind to me,' she said.

'Put this on.' Jade handed her the black shirt. She stood. She watched Yvonne slip it on. 'Use the belt.'

'I have no pants.' Yvonne slipped the belt down to her hips.

'What are you going to wear?' Yvonne asked.

Jade took the thermal vest from her bag.

'In my bag you'll find combs, brushes, make-up, though you don't need any. Help yourself.'

The girl ran her hand down the length of Jade's hair.

'I have never seen hair so long,' she said.

'What on earth made you sleep like that?'

The girl brushed her hair. She looked at herself in the mirror and swished it this way and that.

'Never in my life have I worn black,' she said.

'It suits you,' Jade said. She slipped on the thermal vest and folded the table-cloth to make a shawl. She slung it around her and secured it on one shoulder with a clasp.

'Let me brush your hair,' the girl said. She ran the brush through Jade's hair until it stood out with life around Jade's body.

'You are beautiful,' Yvonne said.

Jade looked at her. 'Now,' she said. 'Who would know?'

Yvonne collected her dress from the window. Jade wiped out the last basin. She took some perfume oil from her bag and unscrewed the top.

'Stand still,' she said. She lifted Yvonne's hair away from her shoulders at the nape and put the perfume on her neck and behind her ears. She held Yvonne's hand and put the perfume on her wrist. She touched the oil on her temples.

'There,' she said. 'Who would know?'

She put the bottle back in her bag. Yvonne's hand caressed her hair. The bins had to be dragged back. The door was heavy. They walked out into the sunshine.

'I knew there wasn't no breakdown. Dirty girls. I knew you was up to your shenanigans.'

They were accosted by a very tall thickset woman dressed in a Sunday suit. She had a stick with her.

'I could have got a parkie on to you. Dirty girls with your drugs and your dirty ways. I could have got the law on to you.'

The woman's face was red with choler. She pushed between Jade and Yvonne and went into the ladies' toilet to relieve herself.

The gypsy man brought his baby and his dog back to the swing ball. He unstrapped the baby and rolled him on the grass. The dog flopped down. The gypsy man pulled at his black silk ears and carried on playing with the child. John watched. He was still shaking. The gypsy man was lying flat on his back holding the baby above him at arm's length. The baby wavered this way and that; it was laughing.

'Go on, crawl.' The gypsy man put the baby down. It crawled back and forth across his body from one side to the other.

John looked round for Naomi. He couldn't see her.

'Where's . . .' he called.

'Where's Yvonne?' the gypsy man shouted over to John.

'Gone to the loo,' John shouted back. He would have to explain. He stood up. His legs wouldn't walk. He sat down. He smiled at the gypsy man and said nothing.

'I want to go back now,' the child said. Roger heaved himself up on to his feet. One or two roses were spreading their hearts bare in the rose garden, most were buds.

'Don't like roses,' Roger said. 'They're ugly when they fade.'

'Naomi likes roses,' the boy said. 'Can we go back now? My daddy might be worrying.'

'You're with me,' Roger said. He was tired. His face felt sticky. There was still a splash of red on his cheek. He put his hand up to his hair. It was sticky. He ran his fingers through it. His fingers were sticky. He counted the hairs on his hand. Seven.

'I'm moulting,' Roger said.

'Budgies moult,' said the boy.

'I'm losing my feathers,' Roger said. 'I won't be pretty without my plumes.' He tucked the boy's hand into his.

'You're sticky,' the boy said. 'I want to go home.'

Roger put one foot in front of the other. It felt like walking. The ground slid out behind him.

'We're going to roll down the hill,' he said, 'because I promised.'

The boy trotted along at his side.

'Watch where you're going, young man.' Roger had trodden on an old lady's arthritic toe.

'I beg your pardon,' he threw back over his shoulder, smiling his baby bland vacant smile and thinking about dry Martini with lemon and herbs and sitting on the floor cushion in his summer front room. The boy pulled him on.

'Let's run,' he said. 'Let's run to the hill.' Roger lumbered his bulk into a jogging trot. He thought he could feel spots of prickly heat in his armpits. Then after ten yards he could feel nothing but his burning, heaving, panting chest.

'There she is,' the gypsy man yelled. He pointed. John flung his body round. He opened his heart for Naomi. Jade and Yvonne were strolling down the hill, arms linked, exciting attention from the dog masters and the gold clad women. John couldn't bear to watch them.

'Naomi,' he muttered, 'Naomi, come here, woman.'

'There she is,' shouted the gypsy man. 'You've changed your dress,' he yelled. 'Why have you changed your dress, petite?'

John wiped his hands down the sides of his combat trousers. The girl sat down beside them. He could smell her perfume. Her hair brushed his cheek. She put his hand on her leg.

'Feel,' she said. 'I'm warm now.'

John couldn't look at her.

'I'm sorry,' she said. 'It was a ridiculous fuss to make over a kiss.' She said it quietly with her eyes on the gypsy man.

'What happened to your dress?' the gypsy man yelled. He was still playing with the baby.

'I put my foot in the lake. I slipped. It got wet,' she shouted.

'It was a nice dress.' The baby rolled and laughed.

'I washed it out. It's all right.' Yvonne put her hand on John's. 'Please,' she said. 'Do look at me.'

A voice screamed out 'fore' and a hard dog's ball hit John on the side of the head. The woman who followed the ball was hearty and happy, windcheater and shorts.

'No harm done, eh?' She rubbed John's head. 'Retrieve the ball. All's well, eh?' She waited for some sign. John smiled a watery smile.

'Come along, Soo Soo.' A full scale poodle followed her away from the rug.

John rubbed his head. He thought he saw Naomi coming round the lake. It was not. A kerfuffle broke out behind them.

'Oh Lord,' Jade said.

Soo Soo had bitten through a bright brand new football belonging to two distressed small boys.

'Dogs,' they heard the windcheater woman's voice, 'will be dogs. He's a tremendous sweetie when you know him.'

The boys were bawling. Their mother simply held out her hand to the windcheater woman and informed her that the ball cost four pounds and ninety-nine pence as it was a model of Sergeant Major Zero and that two ice-creams would be required to cheer up her screaming children, large ice-creams. The bill, she said, would come to six pounds.

'Oh Lord,' said Jade. 'We've had the best of the day.'

The windcheater lady blustered. John's hand still rested on Yvonne's leg. He hadn't the strength to remove it.

'I'm sorry I kissed you,' he said.

'Where's Roger?' Jade said. 'Where's Naomi? Hey,' she yelled to the gypsy man, 'where's Naomi?'

There came a yelling from the top of the hill. Roger and the boy had arrived. Jade turned round. Yvonne holding tight to John's hand turned too.

'Do look, John,' Jade said.

'Come on Blot, shout,' said Roger. 'Shout louder.' He jumped up and down, waving his arms in the air. 'We want them all to look. The whole world.' He screamed, 'Hey up!'

His foot crushed down on a vagrant sandwich belonging to a neatly clad lady in a sun-hat. It was liver sausage.

'Oh,' she said.

It was the boy who apologized. The noise had taken Roger over. The hill was high, he was hysterically frightened and wanted an audience for his great deed of derring-do. He'd forgotten the boy who had his back turned and was talking to the liver sausage lady. Roger let out a banshee wail. He flung himself flat out on the ground, bouncing on his stomach, bruising twigs and crushing grass. He pushed off with his hands, twisted, raised himself slightly in the air, let go. It was the most exciting moment of his life. Faster. He was the sky. He was the grass. His blood beat in the earth. Roger laughed as he rolled, laughed and laughed. Down at the bottom of the hill, not very large, not very small, down at the bottom of the hill was a stone. Rather a nice stone, prettily marked. A proud stone. The stone sat at the bottom of the hill with Jade and John, Yvonne and the gypsy man. The stone watched Roger roll down the hill.

Roger was laughing at the sunshine. His nose went into the earth, he came round spluttering to face the sky and the sun shot into his eyes like a surprise.

> 'I'm a brave, brave mouse,
> I go marching round the house,
> And I'm not afraid of anything.'

Roger's heart sang to the sun. Long ago, before it occurred to him that he was allowed to roll down hills, Roger and Jade went to a charity cricket match. Jade wore a picture hat and a long dress with a frill round the bottom to clean up the grass. There was a tandoori chicken stand in the corner of the field which also sold chips. Roger had three helpings of both and dropped tandoori chicken sauce all down the front of his white boiler suit. He wiped his greasy hands on the side, on the seam, where the legs became the bum. He was blissfully happy. He scattered his chip papers on the grass, and crushed the polystyrene tandoori chicken containers under his white kid foot. Jade saw and hid behind her hat. Next to the tent was a gypsy tarot lady. A suburban housewife dressed in headscarf and fringes with a lot of eye make-up, but Roger took his greasy palm to her hoping for wisdom and comfort, hoping for this sunny day to set his life right. The palm was read. The suburban housewife, receiver of ill-gotten junior financier's gains, asked Roger in an atrocious imitation of a foreign accent, please to shuffle. She laid out the cards. Jade stood behind Roger, her hands on the back of his chair, tutting at the grease and the state of his romper suit. Roger looked into her beautiful face and called her 'Mary'. The world was silent. The gypsy woman was staring at him. Nothing moved. No word came from the gypsy woman. Roger stared at her. He was shaking. Her hands on the cards were trembling. Nothing moved. Roger wanted to scream, couldn't take his eyes from the gypsy woman's face. She was pale, couldn't drag his eyes away. Her lips were pale. Her face was hideous, eyes rimmed in dark and shadows of fear.

'You,' she said, 'you're going to have to be very brave,' in an accent that was pure Barnes Common, the south side. She swept up the cards and turned away. Roger stood up tall in the sunshine, sweat patches under his arms.

'I'm a brave, brave mouse,'

and hit his head on the stone, laughed at the sunshine, and hit his head on the stone, stuck his nose in the grass, the twigs and the earth with his head hit on the stone.

It was time for Naomi to get up but she didn't. The bird had long ago deserted her but she hadn't moved. The wind was blowing into the rhododendron grove but she stayed frozen, just as she was when the gypsy man departed with his dog and his baby. The birds sang in the rhododendron grove and the shadows grew longer, stretched out by the wind. It was cold.

* * *

'Daddy, Daddy, Daddy, Daddy.' The boy hurtled down the hill into his father's arms. John lifted him high and held him close. They stood looking at Roger. Jade knelt at his side.

'Roger, for God's sake Roger don't be so bloody stupid,' she said. 'Get up.'

Roger prone beside the stone had not caused everybody to gather round immediately. They had laughed at the sight of him rolling and rolling faster and faster down the hill and turned away before he reached the bottom. John was anxious for the boy, alone at the top of the hill, isolated by the spectacle of the fat man, his friend, in all his abandonment. Then the quiet had stopped them talking.

'Don't be a fool,' Jade shouted from the rug. 'Come over here.'

John called to the boy.

'Roger,' Jade said, 'you're making me cross.'

The boy stood still at the top of the hill.

'Will you get up,' Jade said and the sight of his bulk messing up the greensward got her to her feet, drove her off the rug and knelt her down at Roger's side.

'Daddy, Daddy, Daddy, Daddy.'

The boy ran down the hill. John flung himself out to catch him.

'That's stick on his head,' said the boy, 'lollipop stick.'

'What?' Jade said.

The boy didn't speak.

'What?' Jade said again.

It was the gypsy man who knelt beside Roger, opposite Jade, put his hand to Roger's head and brought it away covered with blood.

'Roger,' Jade said, still angry.

It was the gypsy man who pointed to the stone.

'Roger, wake up,' Jade said.

Roger was in the land of far dreams and he did not want to come back.

The gypsy man put a hand on Roger's heart.

Roger's dreams had him slim, jogging down a road in a track suit dry of sweat with a gleam of white sweatband at his brow.

The gypsy man kept his hand steady on the great mound

of Roger's breast and felt nothing.

Roger was at the top of his home road, undistressed by a five-mile run, going easily, about to kick out and sprint for home. Roger's torso was lean and hard. Roger's legs were pistons of steel. Roger kicked. The rhythm of his feet changed. He pounded into the pavement, sprang off in his bright white training shoes with not a hint of dog shit on the soles. Roger stretched out, faster, faster. Hardly breathing, moving nothing but the great pistons of his legs, no excess movement, no rolling, no distress. He pulled up at his own front door to see Jade awaiting him, Jade applauding him, Jade carrying his child inside her beautiful body. It was full summer and he looked up at the homely flat with its blowing curtains. He put his hand on his heart. He was undistressed, panting slightly, heart beating strongly.

The gypsy man put his ear to Roger's chest.

'For God's sake, Roger,' Jade said. Yvonne was cradling her, soothing her, taking the bad temper out of her.

'He's all right,' the gypsy man said and Roger opened his eyes.

'Oh,' he said. 'Sorry.' He tried to get up. 'I'm awfully tired, you know. Awfully tired.'

A huge beetle crawled over Naomi's hand. It was bright black. Its antlers shone out from its head. It crawled up onto Naomi's hand and off the other side, without the hand responding in any way. The wind blew the hem of the skirt back, exposing an edge of lace on the white petticoat. The lace had belonged to Naomi's grandmother. It was hand-sewn onto the cotton of the petticoat. A ladybird got caught in its web and freed itself immediately. It pulled itself out onto the cotton and flew off home.

They dragged Roger onto his feet and sat him down on the rug. He felt sick and Jade placed a plastic bowl at his side.

'I'm going to be sick, Blot,' Roger said and he started to cry. Jade dropped Rescue Remedy into his lolling mouth and sent Yvonne with another plastic picnic bowl to bring water from the wistaria hut. John cuddled the boy and the gypsy man smiled upon them all. Jade used her wet cloth on Roger's face.

'It was a nice dream,' Roger said and he cried some more.

'Take him to the hospital,' the gypsy man said.

'Where is she?'

'I'm so sorry,' the gypsy man said.

'Where is she?' John was speaking very quietly.

'I left her over there,' the gypsy man pointed. 'She was quite happy to be alone.'

John stood up with the child.

'Leave the child with me,' the gypsy man said. 'I will see no harm comes to him.' His own child was asleep once more, strapped in the pushchair, the dog was on guard and the swing ball in bits and strapped into a bundle.

'I'll take him,' John said.

'As you wish.'

Jade tore a strip from the damask table-cloth to bind her husband's head. When that was done, he felt stronger. He saw himself floating into the harbour of a sacred isle, wounded and attended by queens. Yvonne knelt by him with a bowl of water and majestically he dipped his fingers in and consented to dry them on what was left of the table-cloth.

'I'm sorry,' the boy said. He was on John's back climbing the hill at the beginning of the quest for Naomi.

'Wasn't your fault,' John said. They reached the top of the hill.

'You'll have to walk,' John said. He let the boy down onto the ground, where he stood with bowed head.

'I'm tired,' John said. 'I'm bone weary.' He put his arm round the boy's shoulders and couldn't make up his mind which way to go.

'When can we go home?'

John turned right, guided by a red flush of rhododendrons.

'We've got to find Mummy,' he said.

* * *

'I'm fine, absolutely fine.'

'Don't look at me like that,' Jade said.

Roger had been studying her, staring, eyeing her face, ever since she had bound up his forehead.

'We're quite wrong, you know,' he said, 'quite, quite wrong.'

Yvonne put her arm round Jade's shoulder.

'Would you like it that we drive you home?' she said, offering the gypsy man's services. She stroked Jade's brow.

'Mary,' Roger said, 'Mary.'

Jade turned her face away from him and twisted a long strand of hair over her shoulder to shade herself from his eyes.

'I can do that for myself, I thank you very kindly,' said Roger. 'Myself and those for whom I am responsible. I can see us home.'

The gypsy man stood up. 'We will go,' he said. 'It is time we fed my little son. If you are sure you need no help we will go home.'

Jade put her arm round Yvonne's neck.

'You must keep the shirt,' she said.

'Give me your address,' Yvonne said. 'I will return it to you.'

'Mondays and Fridays she's without me at home,' Roger said.

The gypsy man bowed. No address was given and Yvonne took the dog lead and walked away. The gypsy man smiled, picked up his bundle of swing ball kit and pushed his son up the hill towards his home.

'Mary Jade, Jade Mary, Mary Jade, Jade Mary,' Roger chanted softly.

'Are you well enough to drive?'

'Mary, Mary, Mary, Jade, Jade, Jade.'

'You'll have to see a doctor tomorrow.'

He was silent. Jade picked at the grass, plucking out daisies and beheading them.

'Things are going to be different,' Roger said.

Jade was afraid. She muttered almost unheard, 'You must see a doctor.'

'I shall change. Oh yes, I shall change.' He paused. 'You shall change too,' he said.

Jade got up and wandered down to the black water. She heard him behind her shouting, 'Mary, Mary, Mary.'

'I want Mummy,' the boy cried.

John had been dreading that. Round the rocks, the nooks, crannies and wistaria ways they had walked, through rhododendron bushes and once across a stream on stepping-stones. John picked up the boy.

'I want her too,' he said. 'It's been a ridiculous day.'

The boy snuggled down onto his shoulder and forced John to carry him.

'You'll have to get on my back,' John said, 'I can't do it like this.'

The boy laid his head on the back of John's left shoulder and put his arms round John's neck. He fell instantly asleep. John heaved himself up onto his feet and trod on through the byways. His son gave him confidence.

Roger was king. The lake and the picnic hamper were his domain. Tomorrow his reign would begin. Tomorrow would be his coronation day. Crowned with a snow white sweatband, he would proceed to hold sway. He placed a firm hand upon the picnic hamper and threw a majestic eye upon his lady queen promenading at the water's edge in thoughtful mood. She would come under the length and breadth of his understanding.

John passed a narrow entrance to a tangle of rhododendron bushes hard by a litter bin. He thought he saw a blue skirt as he walked past. He walked on. He walked back.

'Naomi,' he called through the entrance. 'Naomi.'

The figure he saw lay very still. He walked into the grove. Her eyes were open. They looked up at the tops of the bushes, at the sky, refused to look at him. The wind had blown her skirt high above her waist but the petticoat, white and lacy, stayed chastely down to cover her. Her legs were crossed at the ankles, one boot upon the other.

'Naomi.'

The grove was very still. Naomi's face was white.

'It's cold, Naomi.'

Naomi's lips were pale.

'It's evening.'

Her hand dug down into the earth. The fingers wriggled and dug among the twigs and leaves. Naomi brought her eyes away from the heavens. She smoothed down her skirt, uncrossed her legs and looked at John.

'I'm stiff,' she said.

'I was worried.'

'My leg's gone to sleep.' She laughed. 'Oh that hurts,' she said and she pummelled life back into it. 'Jesus God, how did it get so cold?'

'What happened to you?'

She pushed herself up onto her feet.

'I've got pins and needles,' she said and stamped up and down the grove, shaking the birds into life, rubbing her arms, rubbing colour back into her face, biting her lips.

'You were a long time.'

'I fell asleep.' She looked around the grove. She kissed John lightly upon the side of the mouth. Placed a gentle hand on the side of her sleeping son's cheek.

'Whatever happened to the gypsy man?' she said.

They did not go directly back to the car. Roger walked six paces in front, bandaged head gleaming in the sun, pale hair blowing, a knight's crest in the breeze; Roger led his men John and the boy, and pack animals Jade and Naomi, through the rose garden and into the pretty wilderness. He led them through nettles, bluebells, whipped them with briars and broke them on the hills. He did not look back once. The others, particularly Mary his wife, made no complaint. Roger strode at a great rate up hill and down dale, his pace was intrepid and his heart was high. He came by chance to the grey and silver BMW. The key leapt to his hand and he ensconced himself in the driving seat, fingers tapping a commanding rhythm on the steering wheel. Fingers drumming, palm drubbing. Jade, his wife, slipped a hand round his stomach and retrieved the key from the ignition. He saw the action but made no remark. The key would be returned to him, he knew. Jade opened the boot and replaced the picnic hamper and the rugs. She shut the boot. She opened the passenger door, slid inside and leaned over to unlock the rear doors so that John and Naomi could get into the back. Roger's eyes rested on her face. Mary, his wife, raised her own eyes shyly to his and read his thought. She unlocked the back door and got out of the front.

'He wants you beside him,' Mary told John. John indicated his sleeping son.

'Your wife will take the boy,' Mary said. 'Please do as my husband asks.'

Mary's voice was low. John gave the child to Naomi who slid with difficulty across the back seat. John sat beside Roger, Jade beside Naomi. There was a pause. Roger banged the steering wheel once with his right palm. Mary, his wife, apologized softly and returned the key to him.

'You shouldn't be driving,' John said.

Roger broke his long silence. He turned his iron-clad glance upon his passenger. 'Can you drive?'

'That's not the point,' John said.

'Can you drive?' Roger's steely eye bored down to John's soul.

'No,' said John.

'That's the point,' said Roger.

'I can,' said Naomi.

'You are in the back seat,' said Roger.

'We could change,' said Naomi.

'Have you ever driven a grey and silver BMW automatic?' said Roger, quite politely.

'I've driven an automatic,' said Naomi.

'This is a BMW,' said Roger. 'A one-man car. Man car. You are in the back seat.'

Roger started the engine.

'It is a young car,' he said. 'A beautiful car.'

Mary, his wife, put her hand on Naomi's arm and looked

at her pleadingly. John stretched his hand out and braced himself on the top of the dashboard. His hand was shaking. Naomi acquiesced, she gave them all her silence. Roger soothed the ruffled feathers of his silver grey BMW by running his hand twice round the steering wheel, then he turned the key in the ignition. The engine did not complain.

'There,' said Roger and slid smoothly out into the traffic. They passed a squared-off boating lake at the top of a hill.

'In the mornings sometimes,' Jade said, 'all the police horses come out from the stables, just down there. They're exercised out on the common land, line upon line of them, half mounted, half on the leading rein. They look superb. Bright brown gleaming horseflesh. There's nothing to match it.' Jade shook out her long mane of hair. 'On the way back the horses are allowed to stand in that boating pond and drink the water. They look beautiful. People have begun a campaign to stop them using it.'

'They piss in the water,' Roger said.

'Petitions and things,' Jade said.

'Children use that pool,' Roger said. 'You can't have children paddling about in horses' piss.'

'People are so petty,' Jade said.

'Do not chatter.' Roger's voice was hard and Mary, his wife, shut her pretty painted mouth.

'Where are we now?' The child was awake.

'Blot,' said Roger, 'is that you, Blot?'

'Where are we?' the boy asked. He pushed off his mother to sit at the window.

'You want to play with my big red car, don't you?' said Roger.

'Yes,' said the boy.

'I'm taking you back to the flat,' Roger said. 'We'll play together, you and me.'

'Good,' said the boy.

John's hand gripped the top of the dashboard. He wanted very badly to take his family home. Naomi shifted on the back seat. There was a sore place in between her legs where the gypsy man had been and so much of his sperm was leaking out that she was afraid she might leave a damp patch with a distinctive odour on the upholstery of Roger's

BMW. Mary Jade put her little finger with exquisitely pointed and painted nail in the corner of her mouth and bit down on it with sharp little teeth. The nail varnish cracked and flaked on her tongue. Mary Jade smiled a beautiful smile.

'Roger,' said the boy, 'I like you.'

John wanted very much to go home.

Roger switched the windscreen wipers on as he sat in the driving seat, parked at the kerb outside his own front door. He had allowed his wife and his two grown-up friends to unpack the car and enter the summer flat before him. The rain splatted down on his silver grey car. The boy crawled into the front seat. Their breath misted up the windscreen. Roger drew a round circle in the mist and gave it two eyes. The boy added curly hair and a smiling mouth. Roger gave it a nose and freckles. Mary Jade stood out in the rain tapping a long-nailed tap on the window of the driver's door. Roger did not bother to wind it down.

'We'll be out when the sun shines.'

He put his arm round the boy's shoulders. His little wife walked demurely away.

'Does it hurt?' the boy asked.

Roger put his hand up to his wounded forehead.

'Yes,' he said.

'Naomi says you should always cry if something hurts a lot,' said the boy.

'It's braver not to,' said Roger.

'Naomi says that's stupid,' said the boy.

'Naomi's a woman,' said Roger.

'I think you're very brave,' said the boy. 'I would have cried.'

'Heroes don't cry,' said Roger.

'Are you a hero?' asked the boy.

'For today,' said Roger.

'Will you be one tomorrow?'

Roger drew a fat figure of a man in the mist. He gave him big ears and a bald head.

'Is that you?' said the boy.

Roger wrote his name underneath.

'Roger,' said the boy.

Jade busied herself in the kitchen. Naomi busied herself in the bathroom. John closed the windows against the deluge and fiddled with the central heating clock pointed out to him by Mary, wife of Roger, the man who liked always to be warm and couldn't stand wool next to his baby skin.

'Neither can my son,' John said.

There was a fishy smell coming from the kitchen. Jade mashed tuna fish in a bowl. Naomi struggled with her own fishy smell in the bathroom. The gypsy man had deposited too much sperm inside her and though she sat on the loo it would not come out faster than it wanted to. She used a cloth and sponge to wash herself. Jade did not have a douche. Naomi washed her knickers out in the sink and squeezed them dry. There was a hair dryer on the shelf above the sink. She pretended her hair had been wet in the thunderburst and turned it on her knickers.

'All right to use your hairdryer?' She didn't wait for an answer.

Jade twisted pepper onto the tuna fish in the bowl. She placed half a lemon onto a Moulinex electric juicer, held it down firmly and tipped the juice into the bowl. She lumped in some Hellman's Mayonnaise and sprinkled paprika. She mashed hard with a fork. She sliced thin some brown bread and slipped it into the toaster. She switched the oven of the Baby Belling very low to keep the toast hot. She put fresh coffee into the percolator and filled it with water. The central heating was on, John had conquered the clock. He stood leaning against the kitchen door.

'I like gadgets,' Jade said, 'the garbage disposal, my juicer. Remind me to give you the Beast.'

She reached into the freezer and lifted out a frozen carton. 'It should be alive,' she said.

She tipped the carton out. White curds caught in frozen water. She turned the percolator on. The toaster popped.

She put the toast in the oven of the Baby Belling. She fetched a tray and placed upon it cups of black china, tall and thin, and matching plates.

'He should see a doctor,' John said. Jade reached scissors from a neat hook. She cut an empty Evian water bottle in half.

'If we put it in here and cover it with this, you should get it back safely,' she said. She put cling film over the top of the half bottle. The suspended curds were inside. The toaster popped.

'Did you hear me?'

Jade put the toast into the oven.

'How many slices?' she said.

'Jade,' John put his hands on her shoulders. 'A doctor.'

'I don't want to make him do anything.'

Naomi slipped damp knickers on under her skirt and immediately felt sperm slip onto them. She left the bathroom. John took his hands from Jade's shoulders.

'There's a patch of blue sky,' Naomi called from the front room to the back. 'They're leaving the car.'

She watched Roger pick her son up and not bother to lock the door of his BMW. Jade pressed the buzzer that opened the front door.

'He's got to see a doctor,' John said.

Roger called up from the bottom.

'Martini,' he said, 'scented, with lemon, herbs and ice and gifted by our own dear friends.'

Roger guided his bum down onto a black cord cushion. He was sweating with the effort of carrying the boy up the stairs. He sat cross-legged upon the cushion and the boy sat beside him. He swirled ice and lemon round in the Martini in a tall glass. Mary, his wife, wafted drinks out for everybody, placed tuna fish, toast and freshly made coffee in the middle of the room and sank gracefully down by her husband's right hand. Silence hit the room. Roger was upon his throne. Roger was surveying his realm. He picked a white thread from the brown carpet.

'I suckled at my mother's breast,' he said. 'How many of our generation can say that?'

'Can I have the car?' the boy asked.

'You suckled, Blot,' Roger said.

'Please,' said the boy.

'She did that for you, your mother, you can be grateful for that,' Roger said. 'A toast to the sucklers and the suckled. Mary, bring Blot the car.'

Mary did exactly as she was told. Brought car and control unit and placed them at the boy's feet. Roger raised his glass.

'To the suckled,' he said. 'I am a very lucky man.' He drank and the others drank with him.

'Standing outside my mother's front door one day in the porch that served as a garage for the car we did not have, I was present when an Indian gentleman in a turban carrying a suitcase walked up the front garden path and rang the doorbell. I was four years old. Very close to my mother. The gentleman was selling clothes. Gaudy articles which would not appeal to my mother at all. Moreover she made it a policy never to buy from gentlemen upon doorsteps, particularly Indian gentlemen. She was uneasy about turbans. When she opened the door the case was already unlocked displaying its silken blouses. My mother said not a word, nor did the Indian gentleman. He beckoned to me. I went to him. He put his hand upon my head. "This child is a lucky child," he said. "He has a bump, just here." And he put his hand on my forehead. "That will see him lucky through life." The Indian gentleman smiled at me and I at him. I liked his turban. My mother was frightened. She knew about the bump, no one else. She bought from the Indian gentleman a bright blue velvet blouse with lace at collar and cuffs and pearl buttons and a lucky charm, a fat little bead with painted blue spots. "Your purse will never be empty," said the Indian gentleman, shut up his case and walked away. My mother grabbed me to her and felt my head all over with her hands. The blouse cost her three pounds. We were poor. She never wore it. "I thought he would curse you," she said. She was also afraid that he had spirited my luck away and so she searched until her fingertips found it. I still have that luck today.' Roger raised his glass.

'I've never used it,' he said. The sweat was glistening on his forehead. He was pale. He got up from the cushion and went to the bathroom. They heard him being sick.

'He should see a doctor,' John said.

'Take the drinks away,' Naomi said. 'He shouldn't drink alcohol. Don't give him any solid food for a couple of days. Camomile tea,' she said.

The boy sent the car buzzing round the room. Then it stopped.

'The batteries have run down,' he said.

Naomi felt guilty. Batteries for remote-controlled vehicles were expensive. She wanted to go home. She wanted not to have bedded the gypsy man. She wanted a bath.

Mary Jade removed the drinks from the room and poured them back into the Martini bottle. The child followed her.

'I'm thirsty,' he said.

Mary Jade cursed friends with children and the expectation that she, childless, would cater for their needs.

'You can have water,' she said. The child shook his head. Mary Jade took two oranges from the fruit bowl and cut them in half. She turned on her Moulinex juicer.

'Watch this,' she said. 'This is interesting.' She pressed the orange half onto the juicer and pushed down. The juicer ground round. She poured the juice into a glass and pressed another half orange on the Moulinex.

'Can I do that?' said the boy.

'Feel free.' Jade stood back. The boy pressed down and the juicer juiced. They poured the juice into the glass.

'This is my toy,' Jade said. 'Do you like it?'

'Yes,' said the boy.

'Of course,' Jade said, 'what we'd really like to do is buy the flat upstairs and make the whole thing into one. It's rented at the moment. It's got a roof garden.'

The boy concentrated on his orange juice. Jade didn't know why she'd said it.

'I'm going to give your mummy the picnic hamper,' she said.

'She likes baskets.'

The boy's juice was ready. Jade poured it into the glass. The boy drank it down in one long gulp.

'I'm still thirsty,' he said.

'Have some water.' Naomi was behind him. Her face was stern. The boy looked at Jade.

'Yes please,' he said.

Roger left the bathroom.

'I'm suffocating,' he said and waded through the front room into the cupboard bedroom to lie down.

'We must go,' Naomi said. 'It's a long way home.'

Mary Jade shoved the yoghurt beast in its improvised canister into her hand.

'I want you to have the picnic hamper,' she said. 'If you don't have it I'll give it to a jumble sale. We've never used it until today. We won't use it again. We have to throw things out living as we do in a shoe box. It would give me great pleasure to give you the picnic basket.'

Naomi leant across. She ran her hands down Mary Jade's bare arms, she touched her fingertips and kissed her cheek.

'I'll use it for my sewing,' she said.

'I thought,' Mary Jade had a sparkling eye, 'I thought you could have used it for picnics.'

She emptied the hamper and passed it to Naomi.

'I've some other things for you,' she said. 'You can take them home in the hamper.'

Mary Jade brought a real sponge from the bathroom, and a jar of Body Shop hair gel. From a drawer in the knocked back fireplace she took a length of silver boob tubing slightly out of fashion, for use under disco lights. She grabbed a copy of *The Far Pavilions* from a top shelf.

'There,' she said. 'Just for fun.'

Naomi accepted the gifts and opened the basket.

'I hope the yoghurt beast's alive,' Mary Jade said.

Naomi was always the recipient of gifts. Friends unasked ransacked jumble sales and brought her unwearable clothes which they said were her kind of thing and never were. She put them up in the loft, being sure that if she gave them to another jumble sale they would only come back to her as the gifts of her collective friends. They gave her plants for her overstocked garden, herbs and lettuces. They gave her cultures to bake cakes with and sunflowers to brighten her soul. Their sons came to play with her son and brought her roses. Women came to tea bearing cabbages and pineapples. Naomi had learnt to accept gifts without fuss. She hated baking and hated cabbage, but faithfully she did what she was supposed to do and saved her soul. Now she had been given a child by a gypsy man.

'We must go home.' John had come into the back room.

'We're going, my love, we're going,' Naomi said, packing her little basket.

'Can I say goodbye to Roger?' The boy looked patiently from one adult to another.

'Yes,' said Mary Jade, 'I think you should.' 'Darling,' she added, because the boy was extremely beautiful.

'Those eyes,' she said as he left the room.

Roger was lying on the bunk divan with his hands crossed on his chest. His eyes were closed. This was a white room and the glare of it hurt even when his head did not have a hole in it. The boy climbed across the bed. Roger opened his eyes and closed them again. He stretched out a hand to the boy.

'Would it be good if I closed the curtains?'

'Yes,' said Roger. The sunset was poking straight in at him. 'It would be much better,' he said. 'Thank you.'

The boy climbed back onto the bed and put his hand in Roger's.

'I was sick,' Roger said.

'I know,' said the boy.

'Did you know,' said Roger, 'that I'm much too fat?'

'Yes,' said the boy.

'I can't run and jump and laugh because I'm too fat,' Roger said. A tear trickled out of his right eye. The boy wiped it away with his hand.

'Blot,' said Roger, 'next time you come I'm going to be different.'

'I like you,' said the Blot.

'Do you know what?' Roger heaved himself up on his elbow. He looked at the boy's hand in his and he kissed the boy's cheek. 'I'm ever so glad you like me,' he said and sank back onto the pillow with his eyes shut. He had stopped crying. The Blot stayed on the bed for a while like Naomi after she'd read the last story. Then he clambered quietly to the door.

'Blot,' Roger's eyes were still closed. He crossed his arms once more upon his breast. 'I'm going to be different.'

The boy blew a kiss into the air, caught it in his hand and threw it to Roger who opened his eyes to catch the kiss upon his lips.

They walked up the road. The boy was walking, John was carrying the picnic hamper. Naomi knew Jade would be standing at the window watching them up the road. She was nervous about travellers at night, would have roused Roger from his sleep to drive them all the way home. Naomi turned the boy round to wave to Jade at the window. She dropped down beside him, arm round his shoulders.

'You were very good today,' she said. 'I like taking you out.'

The boy waved to the figure behind the net curtains.

'Did you like Jade's hair?' Naomi said.

'Yes,' said the boy and he stopped waving. 'I liked Roger,' he said. 'Carry me.' Naomi knelt down and the child clambered up onto her back. She carried him up the hill beside his father and she carried the gypsy man's sperm inside her.

When they reached the tube station the lifts were out of order and they travelled down an endless spiral stairway. At the bottom the tube was miraculously waiting. The boy asked to be taken onto Naomi's lap and snuggled into her like a little baby.

'Once,' John said, 'when the lifts were working here, I travelled down on one with a singing lift man. No train came so I watched the lift going up and down with this man singing hymns.'

'It was on tele,' Naomi said.

'Was it?' said John. 'What was strange was that a man was travelling with him, at the back of the lift, standing there, and he didn't get off the whole time I was watching.'

'Was it a Monday or a Friday?' Naomi asked.

'Monday,' said John.
'Had you come to see Jade on your own?'
'Yes,' said John.
'Perhaps he liked the singing.'
They sat in silence for some time. The child's head was hot against her breast and his curls stuck in points to his forehead. Naomi put a hand on his cheek.
'Is he all right do you think?'
'What did you do with the gypsy man?'
'I went for a walk.'
'He's hot, that's all,' John said and he placed a long tapering finger at the nape of the child's neck, touching his wife's breast as he did so.

Mary Jade turned the central heating off and switched off the lights. The tidying-up had been done. There were no threads on the brown carpet. There was no sign that anyone had visited the flat that day. Tomorrow she would go to Covent Garden and watch the buskers. It was women's week. There was a feminist bookstall and a very old friend Juicy Jasmine was belly dancing. Jade had met Jasmine in the Body Shop buying moisturizer for her stomach to keep it supple. Jade was enamoured of Jasmine, a Jewish girl from Edinburgh who wanted to be a comedienne. Jasmine had a way of scratching her long nails through her thin red hair to her scalp and rasping them to and fro which filled Jade with wonder and delight. Jasmine rolled her cigarettes so thin that her fat Cupid's mouth was permanently pouting for a light and her busy fingernails picked threads of tobacco from the cracks in her lipstick. Juicy Jasmine was an ugly little woman with big breasts who had vowed her body to the service of mankind and mankind had accepted worshipfully, committing heinous sins on the altar of her lack of virginity. Fastidious Jade, chaste Mary, was fascinated and worshipped too at the altar of so much freedom. Jewish Jasmine claimed Judaism to be the religion of this life, claimed it to be total joy. Chaste Mary, brought up in sinful joylessness and living in guilty fear, watched in envy.

* * *

A group of crested adolescents got on to the tube. One, six foot with a great auburn crest and leopard spots on the side of his head, sat down beside John. He was wearing a khaki raincoat, collar turned up, and Naomi squinted round with the boy in her arms to look at him. He was beautiful.

'It is becoming too much,' Naomi thought, 'that I should desire to copulate with very young men.'

Her mind dithered over the lusty child she would bear to this young lion of the British Isles.

'Here, Mister,' the lion growled to John with posh undertones belying the harshness of his street voice.

'Here, Mister,' he said, 'what did you do when you was young?'

The lion disposed himself gracefully on the tube seat. Naomi squinted round and watched John blush and stumble through a bed of rough thoughts.

'I thought,' he said finally, 'I still was young.' He smiled at the lion as if a smile would loosen a lion's jaws.

'My social studies teacher's your age,' said the lion. 'My probation officer's your age.'

'I see,' John said and he adjusted the waist of his combat trousers.

The lion's pride were cheering him on, quietly expecting some real answers, grinning.

'Was you a hippy?' said the lion, silencing chortles from his pride with a gesture.

'I walked around in bare feet,' said John, smiling still in the face of the lion's teeth.

'Peace and love,' said the lion and he raised his two fingers in front of John's smile, in the peace sign, in benediction.

'Man,' said the lion.

'Yes,' said John. 'What's wrong with that?' Smiling brave defiance in the face of his living enemy.

'Member of the Labour Party? Denizen of CND?' said the lion, gentle pussy cat and friendly now.

'Yes,' said John, lulled and no longer smiling, ready to lecture and lead the lion at his heels.

The lion laughed a roaring laugh and his pride laughed with him, and pointed their taloned paws.

They got out at the next stop. John's hand was shaking once more. He held it out to Naomi and she, cradling the sleeping child, didn't have a free hand to comfort him.

At the main-line station as they got off the tube, the child woke up hungry.

'If we've got enough money you can have a hamburger and chips,' Naomi said.

'And a Coke?' The boy had had two slices of bread for lunch and two for supper.

'If we've got enough money.' She set the child on his feet and walked on to the escalator.

'Have you got any money, Daddy?'

John did not hear. The boy tugged at his trousers. John saw a girl on the down escalator with raven hair, long and straight, saw her at a distance and when she came close saw the wrinkles on her face and the white roots showing. The hair uneven and stiff on her shoulders. Yellow miniskirt and white blouse. A whore on a Sunday holiday.

'I really am hungry,' the boy said.

John looked down and smiled into the sad eyes of his young son.

'I'll get you chips and a hamburger,' John said.

'And a Coke.'

'Yes,' said John.

At the top of the escalator Naomi gave the tickets to the boy and he presented them to the ticket lady. He waited for a thank-you from her but someone pushed at him through the ticket gate and he ran to Naomi's side.

'That lady pushed me,' he said.

There was a fat lady, squeezed feet in white summer boots, and dyed blonde hair with a bad perm. Her scalp shone pink on the crown and the rings on her fingers cut into her hands.

'Perhaps she's in a hurry,' Naomi said and put her arm round the boy's shoulders.

'Can I play with Laurie when I get home?'

'It's late,' she said.

'Past my bedtime?'

'Yes,' she said.

'Past Laurie's bedtime?'

'Yes,' she said.

They caught up with John at the top of the second escalator.

'Half an hour till the next train,' he said.

'That's a long time,' said the boy.

He skidded across the floor of the main-line station, came back for Naomi and pulled her with him. He chased pigeons, then remembered the giant one in the sky. He decided to ignore it and chased pigeons again.

Behind him, watching, was a tall nymph with red gold hair curling on her shoulders and a sweet face. She had a large portfolio at her feet and a slender leg. She might have been a model, might have been an artist. John saw her first as she swooped on the boy. She put her hand on his shoulder and turned him to face her. Her fingers were lined with paint, her fingernails were grubby. She squatted at his level.

'You are being cruel,' she said. Then she left the child alone in the middle of the station. John smiled at her and the boy began to cry. Naomi picked him up, not quickly enough. He was afraid.

'I don't like her,' he sobbed into Naomi's hair. 'I don't like her.'

Naomi simply said, 'You mustn't chase pigeons.' And she too smiled at the nymph back leaning against the wall with the portfolio.

'Well,' said the boy, 'you don't know anything.' And he pulled Naomi's hair. Naomi looked at John.

'He's tired,' she said and she uncurled her son's hand and kissed his wet cheek.

'I like you,' she said. 'Don't chase pigeons.'

Naomi saw the red-haired nymph with the gypsy man. She saw long white limbs naked in the rhododendron grove and red gold hair spread out and shining on the mother earth. A girl with a sweet face, virgin sacrifice to the gypsy man.

'A nymph will always beat a madonna,' Naomi said.

'What?'

When they were ordering hamburger and chips, the boy stopped crying. Naomi put him down. He wiped his face on her skirts and blew his nose. He took three straws for his Coke and six paper napkins.

'That's enough,' John said.

When they were back outside John queued for tea for Naomi and himself. The boy stood holding his bag of hamburger and chips.

'You'd better eat them,' Naomi said. She was longing for a chip.

'I'm keeping them for the train.'

'Don't be silly,' said Naomi, 'the train won't be here for half an hour.' The desire for a chip, maybe two, made her cross.

'They're mine,' the boy said. 'I can do what I like.'

'By the time you get on the train they'll be cold and greasy and you won't want them.' She became cruel. 'The ice in your Coke will have melted.'

'I haven't got a hand.' The boy was near to tears again. Naomi relented. She took him across to a group of red plastic seats and sat him down. She pushed a straw through the top of his Coke cup and waited patiently until she could steal a chip without upsetting him.

'Sorry,' she said.

When John brought teas he was followed by a man, not quite drunk, not quite a tramp, not quite dirty. John sat down and gave Naomi the tea. The tramp sat down beside them.

'Name of Seamus,' he said, 'but that won't surprise you.' The man was angry. 'See them,' he said, 'see them there.' He pointed at two men in careful casual clothes, talking to each other and surveying the crowd. 'Every bloody night this week. St Marks,' he said. 'I don't want to give up the drink,' he said. 'I don't want to. What would I give it up for? What for? Answer me that.'

'What age are you,' John said.

'I'm not poor,' said the man. 'My family. My father. We've land in Ireland. A lot of land. I could be all right if I wanted to be. You tell them that. You tell them when they come over here bothering me.'

'Let me get you a cup of tea,' John said.

'It's not tea I want,' said the man. 'Forty. I'm forty years old,' and he looked at John long and he looked at John hard. 'I know you,' he said. 'I know you. Liberal,' he said. 'You'll buy me a cup of tea when for a few pence more you could buy me what I really want. You'll lust after women not your wife but your bright conscience'll not guide your hand to your pocket to buy me a drink. I know you. I know you all.'

'You're a young man,' John said. 'You're killing yourself.'

The man shuffled off and spat at the feet of the men from St Marks. John looked at Naomi and shrugged.

'What came over you?' she said, 'you don't usually talk to them. Do you?' she said. 'Do you lust after women not your wife?'

John smiled.

When the train went up on the board the boy handed Naomi the end of a bag of cold chips. 'You can have these,' he said.

The hamburger was gone and he was fishing in the paper cup for the stubs of ice cubes to suck. Naomi took the chips and stuffed the soggy, salty mess into her mouth. John went through all his pockets to find the tickets home.

Mary Jade wandered through the night flat at home and alone. Her ablutions were before her. The pleasure of her fine body in the long bathroom mirror. She went out onto the balcony garden and didn't think of Roger. She breathed in the night smell of a city after rain and tried to catch the fragrance of herbs and earth. For Jasmine she would dress in pale blue, demure, and wear her hair back in a single plait, schoolgirl style. Once Jasmine had had a baby son and called him after an archangel. She had made a present of him to her childless sister and taken up residence in a deserted cinema. Mary Jade had visited her there. The bed was in the orchestra pit.

Jade closed the balcony doors, locked them tight, double-locked the front door, went to the bathroom and peed in the pan with the door wide open. She fixed a rubber nozzle on the bath tap and sprayed herself all alone on the loo. Dip dab. Dip dab. She dried herself on a fresh white towel. She removed her thermal vest and examined her virgin body in the mirror above the sink. She splashed her breasts with cold water and touched the nipple where a mouth should have been. She dried her breasts on the fresh white towel. Neck and ears carefully tended. Mary Jade washed her beautiful face, smoothed out the line of fur on her eyebrows, examined the skin for blemishes and finding none used a toothbrush on her carefully crowned teeth entirely free of gum disease. With the tips of her fingers she worked moisturizer into her face and would not permit Roger to cross the threshold of her mind. She rubbed coconut oil into the ends of her hair and took the brush through it and through it until the world was only Jade's hair and the bathroom did not exist. Jasmine loved her hair. Jasmine said a belly dancer should have hair like hers and threatened to cut it off with the open razor she used as a prop when she dressed as a man and sang in a barber shop quartet. She and Jasmine were always civilized when they met and talked of men and children. Occasionally Jasmine threw her a languishing look from behind round gold spectacles, a look which Jade treasured in virgin isolation in Roger's bed.

'Jade hasn't changed since we were at school.' They were sitting in a non-smoker at the end of the train. The child had insisted on walking up the platform as far as he could go though they were all tired and the picnic hamper very heavy. He still had his cup, empty of Coke and rattling with ice cubes.

'How can someone not change at all?'

John was silent, contemplating the drunken man's aspersions on his lack of morality.

'There isn't a line on her face.'

An ice cube slithered out of the boy's mouth, down his T-shirt and to the floor of the train. John wiped his face with a handkerchief.

'Sorry,' said the boy.

John ran a soft hand over the boy's hair.

'Carry on,' he said and left a soft hand on the boy's shoulder.

'She's beautiful,' Naomi said and bit her teeth into her bottom lip and rubbed at her cheeks to give them colour.

'Don't,' John said.

A fat man in the seat behind lit up a cigarette in the non-smoking compartment. He was politely very drunk and wore an MCC tie. He stared at Naomi. She looked away and fluffed her hair out. She made moon eyes at her reflection in the dark window. Some men found her beautiful. The gypsy man took her in the rhododendron grove. She bit her lip again and made it hurt. The fat man stared and wheezed on his cigarette.

'Roger looked ill,' John said.

'He hit his head,' Naomi said.

'Before that.'

'Is Roger going to die?' The boy was listening avidly, quiet, breathing softly, moving no limb so that his parents would delve into the mysteries of the adult world and reveal its secrets.

'No,' John said. 'He carries too much weight.'

'He's sad,' the child said.

'He's fat,' Naomi said.

The fat MCC man was staring at her with all the courage of a man of good class who's had too much to drink.

'He should go to hospital with that head.' Naomi bent, pulled her skirts back and retied the lace of her boot, showing the fat man the lace on her petticoat. She could smell the gypsy man.

'Madame,' the fat man called, touched to the heart by petticoats edged with lace. 'Madame, you are beautiful.'

John looked round at the fat man behind him, looked back to his wife. The boy looked round at the fat man talking to his mother.

'Do you know him?' the boy said.

'No,' said Naomi and smiled at the fat man then looked coolly into the dark glass.

'Don't smile,' John said.

Naomi winked at him and whispered, laughing, 'I wish he'd called me Mademoiselle.'

'What does that mean?' said the boy.

'When do I get to be a woman?' Naomi asked.

'Madame,' the fat man called. He wobbled up the train, cigarette trailing smoke. He stood swaying at their seats, fumbling at an inside pocket.

'Madame, I mean no disrespect, you are in the protected bosom of your family. I mean you no harm. You are beautiful. If ever you should need me. At any time. If ever I should be able to render you any assistance. I am entirely at your service.' He handed her a card.

'Thank you,' Naomi said and accepted it graciously. The fat man wobbled off the train.

'Why did you take it?' John said.

'It would have been awfully rude not to,' Naomi said. She put the card carefully in her shoulder bag, in the front pouch so that it would be safe.

'Why are you keeping it?' John said.

'He gave it to me.'

'You don't have to keep it.'

'Here,' Naomi said. She handed John the card. He tore it into tiny shreds and sat blushing, his still eyes searching the world for something to do right.

'Are you angry?' said the child. John refused to answer. He gripped his hands together to stop them shaking.

'Is Daddy angry?' the boy asked.

'No,' said Naomi, 'I don't think he is.'

She smiled at John and felt the gypsy man inside her.

Roger lay quite still in the darkness with his eyes open. He contemplated his body in minute detail. He had a corn on the fourth toe of his left foot. He sent his hands out to wander over the softness of his loins and thighs. They gripped into the flab of his sides and pulled out handfuls of white slug skin. Roger's body encompassed the bed he was in. Folds of flesh wandered out and engulfed it. Roger's body took over the room. It was all inside him. He was going to invade the flat with the whole flab of his being when Jade opened the door and he became Roger lying on the bed, calm hands folded across his chest. Jade climbed softly between the sheets. She made sure no part of her body touched any part of Roger's.

'I'm not asleep,' Roger said.

Jade sighed and reached out her hand to switch on the light.

'Don't put the light on,' Roger said.

Jade took her hand back again.

'Are you all right?' she asked.

Roger touched his hand on Jade's thigh.

'Mary,' he said. 'Mary.'

Jade Mary, Mary Jade hoped he wouldn't cry and reached her own hand down to his upon her thigh.

'Go to sleep,' she said. 'It'll do you good.'

'Mary, Mary. I've got my clothes on.'

Mary Jade switched on the light and looked upon her husband sweat-stained, blood-stained and covered in tears lying beside her.

'You can't spend the night like that.'

'No,' he said.

'Come on,' she said. She helped him out across the bed. She helped him through the summer flat and took him into the bathroom to bathe his body and tend his wound.

'What did you do with the gypsy man?' John said.

'He was a toy maker,' said Naomi.

'My kind of toys?' asked the boy.

'No,' said Naomi.

'Where are we now?' said the boy.

The train had stopped at a dark station, platform on one side, none on the other.

'It's that funny station,' said Naomi.

'Why is it funny?' said the boy.

'I don't know,' Naomi said.

The boy changed seats. He sat beside his mother still clutching the empty Coke cup.

'Where shall I put this?' he said. Naomi took the cup from him and chucked it under the seat. She looked at John to see if he minded. John shrugged. She put her arm round the boy and cuddled him in.

'Tired?' she asked.

'No,' said the boy.

'Are you going to tell me?' John asked.

'What?' Naomi smiled at John but didn't have a free hand to hold out to him. 'Yes,' she said. 'I'll tell you later.'

'Let's have a family cuddle,' said the boy.

John moved across. They sat three to a seat, close together, arms entwined.

'You made that man give you the card,' John said.

Naomi smiled at him.

'Why did you do it?'

'Long ago,' she said, 'people would have looked at my age and said that my best years of child bearing were over.'

'People didn't live so long.'

'My hair's going grey.'

'You look young.'

'That's not really the point. I'm not young, John. There's not much time left. I've been very patient.' She smiled at him but he wouldn't smile back. So they sat there quiet, arms entwined.

Roger, bare, confronted himself in the bathroom mirror. He leaned both hands on the basin supporting himself, feet apart, while Jade Mary washed him with a soft sponge from head to toe. Save for the binding round the wound on his head. She took the sponge down his legs, back, inside, outside, front. She ran her hand down his shin and picked up each foot. She pulled the sponge between each toe. Her hair tickled him and he laughed at himself in the mirror. His skin pricked and jagged as the water dried in.

'Dry me, dry me,' he said and she dragged a rough towel up and down his legs taking the itch away. She rubbed lotion into them. Changed the water, started on his body. She rubbed and rubbed soap into the sponge until it was foaming white. Round and round she took it over his great buttocks, up his back, rubbing, the shoulders, down his arms, leaning on the basin, into the armpits, down his sides and round to the front. She stood behind him panting, her face flushed with effort. He smiled at her in the mirror and she washed his great stomach and his woman's breasts. His skin was prickling and itching. She rinsed him off, flung a towel round him, soaped the sponge once more.

'Do that yourself,' she said, pointing, 'and when you're finished, come through.'

He rubbed at himself forlornly, rinsed off. All alone in the bathroom, the place untidy, water on the floor. She'd forgotten to put the lotion on his body. He used the towel to mop up the floor, wipe round the sink. He put it with the rest for washing and went naked to find Jade.

The cushion was in the middle of the floor in the back room. Jade had a red plastic bowl of water and another sponge.

'Sit here,' she said.

And he did, crosslegged on the big cushion, pulling his feet in as far as they would go. She cut the binding round his head with scissors, taking some of his hair with it. She peeled the bandage off and he bit his lip so that he wouldn't annoy her by expressing his pain. She bathed the hurt place first, then took the sponge over his face, round his neck, in and out of his ears. She was not gentle when she dried him.

'Will you comb my hair?'

She went to the bathroom to get his own comb and tugged it through his hair. Then she finished.

'You look better,' she said and handed him the comb.

'Aren't you going to bandage my head?' he said.

'It doesn't need it,' and she left him sitting in the middle of the room on the big floor cushion. He heard her wash her hands in the bathroom, spray her face, turn out the light and go to bed.

'Mary,' he said. 'Mary.' There was no reply.

Roger counted the hairs in the comb. They numbered seventeen. Roger put the hairs in the waste disposal in the kitchen, emptied the red plastic bowl, cleaned it out, put his comb back in the bathroom, caught sight of the wound in his head and decided that he really had to think. He shut the back room door and returned to the big floor cushion.

Roger wanted a child. He did not want a child of this great fat body. Roger had to decide what to do.

*   *   *

'Do you think Baashi's will be open?' Naomi asked as they got down from the train.

'It's ten o'clock,' John said.

'That's past my bedtime,' said the boy. 'Can I have two minutes to play when we get in?'

John handed the tickets to the boy. The boy handed the tickets to the man at the gate.

'Yes,' said Naomi.

'No,' said John at one and the same time.

'I want a bottle of Perrier water,' said Naomi. 'Have we got enough money?'

'Yes,' said John.

'Do you mind?' asked Naomi.

'No,' said John.

Naomi bent down and the boy climbed onto her back. She strode out quickly and John swung along to keep up with her.

'I didn't really enjoy it,' she said.

'What?' John asked.

'Today,' she said and hoiked the boy further up onto her back.

'You had a good long sleep,' John said.

'I must have been tired.'

In front of them an old turbanned Indian was walking a dog. He bade Naomi a good evening.

'Who's that?' John said.

'Means Baashi's must be closed,' Naomi said. 'I'm sweating. I need a bath.' A little more of the gypsy man trickled out of her. 'John,' she said, 'do you love me?'

'Yes,' he said.

'Do you?' she said to the boy.

'Yes,' he said.

The lights of Baashi's were still on so she knocked on the door and the tall young Indian with the broad shoulders and the beard unlocked it and let her have a bottle of Perrier water.

'Put it in the hamper,' she said to John.

'Can I have a play?' said the boy.

'Yes,' John said.

'No,' said Naomi at exactly the same time. 'If you have

a wash and you get into your pyjamas with absolutely no fuss, then you can have a play while I have a bath.'

'Who's taking me to bed?' the boy said.

'After my bath,' said Naomi.

And John said, 'I'm dying for a cup of tea.' He shifted the picnic hamper from hand to hand. 'We didn't really need another basket.'

'I like it,' Naomi said. 'It was kind of Jade to give it to us.' And she strode on up the road with the boy bouncing on her back.

'You know,' she said, 'I have decided to get pregnant.' John was too far away to hear and the boy paid no attention.

Roger's eyes stared heavily before him. In the room, in every available space, in each corner, crushing up to the very edge of his cushion were fat women, daring him to look, daring him to touch. One had her breasts exposed dripping down to her waist. She was pushing through the crowd, trying to get to him. He could smell her smell. Her skin was white and oozing. Roger thanked God for the towel round her waist. Her hair was thin on the top of her head and tied back into a greasy pony tail. Her thighs rubbed together, great blue veins, royal rivers of blood, roped down her legs. Roger stared ahead. She got him. The cries of the other fatsos whooped up to frenzy around the cushion. The woman removed the towel from her waist. Roger screamed. Jade Mary heard, lying on the bed in the summer flat, and left him to the contemplation of his fat man's soul. Roger's voice stifled in the fat woman's flesh as she raped his soft open body.

It was full dark. The back room was empty but for Roger, cross-legged on his cushion. It was midnight. Roger got up, he crept through the night flat to the cupboard in the hall and removed a clean dry track suit. It was pale grey. He picked up cotton socks and trainers. Fresh cotton socks, washed by Jade in the kitchen sink. White cotton socks, white trainers. He took scissors out of the kitchen drawer. He cut the neck from the track-suit top. He placed it, sweatband and bandage round his wound. He pulled on the trousers, they were tight round his waist and tight on his bum. He tied on the shoes and eased the track-suit top over his head. It was tight on his breast. Without looking in the bathroom glass Roger left the flat. He strode downstairs and left the building.

The front gate squeaked as John pushed it open. The mock orange blossom threw its heavy scent across at him.

'Who needs a front-door bell?' he said as the gate squeaked back behind Naomi.

'That's always annoyed you,' she said.

'I come home one night,' he said. 'You've cut the wires on the front-door bell, you've pulled the wires from a wall plug and left them bare.'

'They were ugly. The plug was ugly.'

'All the electricity in the house was on. You could have killed yourself.'

'Was I here then?' said the child.

'You can't wait for anything. You can't discuss. Something comes up your back, you do it. Sod the bloody consequences.'

'It was a long time ago.'

'Was it?' John said.

'Are you angry?' said the boy.

'It's your turn to wash him,' John said and he closed the front door.

'Come on,' said Naomi. She and the boy walked through the house to the bathroom.

'Our house is very big,' said the boy.

They heard John throw the picnic hamper into a corner of the front room.

'He'll hit my Lego castle,' said the boy.

'He'll tear the wallpaper,' said Naomi.

She soaped a cloth and washed the boy's face and hands.

'That'll do,' she said. They heard John throw a plastic toy at the wall.

'What was that?' said Naomi.

'Playmobile men,' said the boy.

'You should put your toys away. Don't bite the toothbrush. Clean your teeth.'

The boy scrubbed at his teeth much too hard. John was humming in the front room.

'Don't hum,' Naomi shouted at him. He only sang when he was cross, Simon and Garfunkel, 'For Emily Wherever I May Find Her', sadly as though he never had. Naomi hated Emily.

'You take me to bed,' the boy said.

'Yes,' Naomi said.

'What were you doing visiting Jade on your own?' she yelled at John but there was no reply.

'You get my apple,' said the boy.

'You get your pyjamas on,' said Naomi.

'No,' he said. 'I'll sleep without.' And Naomi was too tired to argue.

'You were going to have a bath,' he said, but Naomi was too tired for that too.

She cuddled her naked son in his wooden bunk. The boy munched an apple and the father hummed on the sofa in the front room.

'Do you want a story?' she said but her eyes were closing. The boy handed her the apple core.

'No,' he said. He snuggled his bum into her and fell asleep.

Mary Jade punched the pillow with a forlorn fist. She'd come to bed much too early. She felt restless and itchy. The room was suffocatingly dark. Mary Jade jumped out of bed and pulled back the curtains. The street lamp prodded her back to bed with its old shaky fingers. Mary Jade slept with nothing on and struggled with the dream that the two poofs in the flat directly across from her bedroom window spent their lives with binoculars to their tired eyes spying for a glimpse of her beauty. One was Irish and a navvy, the other was elderly and had been a weather forecaster. He now made a living drawing birth charts in illuminated script, commissioned by the high and mighty. Jade slipped under the covers and punched back at the pillow. The itch was still there. Between her legs, up a bit. She scrumped up and down in the bed. Strands of hair got into her mouth. She spat them out and stuffed the pillow between her legs. The cool of the pillow eased the itch somewhat. Mary Jade decided that the two poofs across the road had infra-red binoculars and could see her right there in the bed, could see whatever she did. She pulled the pillow out from between her legs and placed it behind her head. She lay still beneath the duvet cover, hair sprayed out across the pillow, hands placed finger to thumb in buddha rings where the fold of the crutch met the pubic hair. A calm Jade and still, but the itch returned. It spread from between her legs and reached her brain. Under the eye of the old poof across the road Jade tried to keep still but Mary wouldn't let her. Mary's hands moved on Jade's thighs. Mary's hands stroked Jade's skin with little circular finger brush strokes. Mary's hands moved gently inwards so's not to frighten Jade. One of Mary's fingers slipped inside Jade and lay very still. Jade felt Mary's finger stay, she thought of the old poof at the window across the way and let the finger stay, she thought of Roger in the back room and let the finger stay. Mary moved the finger inside Jade and slipped another finger in to join it. Mary's other hand cupped Jade's breast and one finger played with the nipple where a mouth should have been. Roger screamed in the back room. Mary spoke to Jade, Jade spoke to Mary and together they decided to let him be. Mary's clever fingers never ceased their butterfly kisses, not for a moment.

When Naomi woke up John was bending over her. She screamed but it didn't wake the child.

'Come on,' he said and walked straight out of the room. He threw himself on the sofa in the front room and hummed the Hymn of Joy.

'What the hell did you scream for?' He broke off the humming to say that.

'What the hell's wrong with you?' She picked up the picnic hamper and took it into the kitchen. The Hymn of Joy flooded the house. Naomi took out the yoghurt beast. It was already unfrozen.

'Must have been hot today,' she called through. She strained the water from the beast and put it into a clay jug.

'You wouldn't know,' he stabbed at her. 'You missed today,' he thrust at her. 'Stolen away by a gypsy man.' He brought the Hymn of Joy through from the front room into the kitchen and stood watching her pour low-fat milk onto the beast in the clay jug.

'Bloody waste of time. Bloody thing's dead,' he said. 'Nothing could live with them.' He blasted the Hymn of Joy full in her face.

'No harm trying,' she said. A smell of coconut wafted out as she opened the jar of Body Shop hair gel.

'That's nice,' she said.

'What did you do with the gypsy man?'

She smoothed hair gel into the front of her hair, teased at it with her fingers and stared at herself in the mirror.

'He called me Madonna and I let him make love to me then I fell asleep.'

Roger was standing with his back against his own front door. He was afraid of the dark.

John burst out laughing.

Mary's fingers pushed further and further into Jade.

'What the bloody hell are you laughing at?'

Naomi's hair was standing up in spikes.

'If you can visit Jade alone on a day when she's in, I can make love with a gypsy man.'

'You look wonderful,' John said.

'Don't.' John put his arms round Naomi.

'I made love with the gypsy man,' she insisted.

'I did not make love with Jade,' John said. 'There now. Is that all right?'

'You don't believe me.'

'Come to bed.'
'I want a baby.'
John pulled her away from the kitchen.
'I'm thirty-three. I want another baby now.'
John put out the light.

John took her upstairs and did not let her undress. He took all his clothes off and made love to her with her boots on. He did not withdraw. His sperm shot up into her and he fell asleep. She felt the sperm wriggling up inside her.

'Ah well,' she thought, 'let them race for it.' She clenched her thighs tight so that nothing ran out.

Roger decided that street lights in a town at night did not constitute darkness. It was cool. He walked down onto the pavement of the summer night. The street was empty. One light in the window of the two poofs across the road, a faint sound of music and voices coming from there. Roger faced up the hill. He put one foot in front of the other and plodded slowly forward.

Mary's fingers played with Jade, teased her. There was sweat on Jade's brow and her hair clamped matted to her forehead. Jade was wet where once she had been dry. Mary smiled reassuringly into Jade's faraway eyes.

Down in the kitchen, inside the clay jug, underneath the milk, the beast lay still and waited.

Naomi pushed John away. He rolled over and she kissed his left shoulderblade. She rolled out of bed being careful not to stand up. She lay flat on the floor on her back, pushed up and did a shoulder stand so that all the sperm cocktail of gypsy man and John would slip far into her.

'Go on,' she said. 'Run.'

'Ducks,' said the boy in the bedroom muttering in his sleep.

Roger quickened his pace. The hair was lifting off the back of his neck. He stretched each foot from heel to toe as he put it down on the pavement and lifted it off. The muscles in Roger's legs smiled. Roger was striding up the hill.

Naomi brought her legs down onto the bedroom floor. Still without standing up, she undid the laces on her boots and kicked them off. Rolling to and fro she slid off underskirt, skirt and top, eased out of tights already at her knees and wriggled out of knickers not removed by either man. She oozed her shoulders onto the bed and let her bum follow. Flat on her back in the yoga corpse position she sent her thoughts out to the sperm jiggling about inside her.
  'Run you buggers. Run.'

Jade Mary. Mary Jade, panting, had an orgasm. The first of her life. The old poof across the road put down his infra-red binoculars smiled at his Irish navvy friend and switched out the light.

In the kitchen the yoghurt beast bubbled and smiled.

Mary Jade fell asleep.

John's hand searched out Naomi's. She kissed his long tapering fingers, snuggled into him, crutch to bum, and fell asleep.

Roger let the pace take him. Sweat prickled out from under his arms and it felt good.
  'Easy,' he told himself. 'Easy. Don't kill yourself, Roger. Easy.'
  His feet fell in a rhythm on the pavement and slowly, slowly, Roger jogged, and slowly, slowly, Roger smiled.